JOURNEY INTO TERROR

The first exploratory expedition to Pluto returns with the Captain, Jules Carmodine, alone . . . What happened to the crew remains a mystery as Carmodine is suffering from amnesia, and mentally and physically broken in health. Later, although his health improves, the amnesia remains. Then, when Carmodine is forced to return to Pluto, he faces a journey into terror. He must remember what happened on that first mission — otherwise the second expedition will suffer exactly the same fate as the first . . .

Books by E. C. Tubb
in the Linford Mystery Library:

ASSIGNMENT NEW YORK
THE POSSESSED
THE LIFE BUYER
DEAD WEIGHT
DEATH IS A DREAM
MOON BASE
FEAR OF STRANGERS
TIDE OF DEATH
FOOTSTEPS OF ANGELS
THE SPACE-BORN
SECRET OF THE TOWERS
THE PRICE OF FREEDOM
WORLD IN TORMENT
THE RESURRECTED MAN
THE GREEN HELIX
THE FREEDOM ARMY

E. C. TUBB

JOURNEY INTO TERROR

Complete and Unabridged

LINFORD
Leicester

First published in Great Britain

First Linford Edition
published 2009

British Library CIP Data

Tubb, E. C.
  Journey into terror
  1. Outer space- -Exploration- -Fiction.
  2. Amnesiacs- -Fiction. 3. Science fiction.
  4. Large type books.
  I. Title II. Tubb, E. C. Alien life.
  823.9′14–dc22

  ISBN 978–1–84782–683–1

Published by
F. A. Thorpe (Publishing)
Anstey, Leicestershire

Set by Words & Graphics Ltd.
Anstey, Leicestershire
Printed and bound in Great Britain by
T. J. International Ltd., Padstow, Cornwall

This book is printed on acid-free paper

1

The deserter

They found him in Crater 4, the festering wound in the heart of the Mato Grosso where the early ships had sprayed the area with radioactives from their dirty atomic exhausts and mutated flora and fauna alike.

The village was a straggle of huts and sheds all sheltering beneath the grotesque trees in a deliberate search for shadow. Even the noon sun did little more than generate a golden haze between rare shafts of penetrating brilliance. It was a place of mystery, disturbing, enigmatic, brooding in the humid silence.

The officer didn't like it. 'How much further?' he demanded. He sounded petulant, irritated at having been selected for this mission.

'Not so far, sir.'

Something moved in the dimness to

one side of the path.

'You pay now, please?' The voice sounded as if it came from a lipless mouth.

'When we see him.' The officer didn't turn to stare at the informer. One glance back at the edge of the clearing had been enough. 'Where is he?'

'In tavern, sir. Always in tavern. You pay me now, please?'

'When we find him.'

He was sprawled across a table in a low-roofed structure set tight against the bole of a tree, a place of knighted dimness and kindly shadow in which distorted figures sat drinking and inhaling plumes of acrid smoke. Around him, on table and floor, rested a litter of empty bottles that had once contained wine.

'God!' whispered one of the guards. 'Is that what we've come to collect?'

He was filthy. His clothes were of synthetic fibre and could not rot but they were torn, stained, fouled with slime and vomit. His hair and beard were a matted refuge for vermin. He had been a physically big man. He was still big in his degradation. His health was gone, his hope, his pride and self-respect. Only an animal sense of caution remained, an instinctive awareness of danger so that his hand groped for an empty bottle as the guards approached.

'Halt!' The officer stepped ahead of his men. He was young and inclined to be censorious. Distastefully he stared at the ruined hulk. 'You there! Wake and listen!'

He opened his eyes. They were crusted with sticky exhudations, bloodshot, yellow with fever, bright with the smouldering fires of madness.

'Doctor Jules Carmodine,' snapped the officer officiously. 'You will rise and accompany me.' And then, as the man made no response, 'Understand me, Carmodine! You are under arrest on a capital charge! Obey!'

Carmodine threw the bottle into his face.

It hit with a splintering thud, landing where the nose joins the forehead, shattering in a spray of fragments. Even as it left his hand, Carmodine lunged forward, overturning the table as he made for the door. The guards were in the way. He shouldered the officer aside and fought with the insensate fury of a trapped beast, using head, hands, knees, elbows, kicking and biting with all the desperate cunning of an animal and all the reactive skill of ingrained training. Then the heavy butt of a gun slammed against his temple and he could fight no more.

They took him to Brasilia, to the big hospital, the operating theatre and therapy rooms. They cleansed his body and healed his wounds. They gave him deep-sleep and intravenous feeding, freed him of parasites and afflictions, weakness and additions and did what they could for his mind. After a long while, they transferred him to jail, and there, left him alone.

Waiting to stand trial for his life.

The irony of it amused him. He savoured it while lying on the narrow cot, staring at the smooth plastic of the ceiling that was mottled with sunlight by day and the water-reflection of Moon and stars at night. It was part of the crazy illogic of Mankind that they should insist on

4

healing a man before ceremoniously killing him. Curing his ailments, rather, for they hadn't been able to effect a complete recovery.

Somehow, somewhere, he had lost a part of his life.

He twisted a little on the hard bunk, suddenly impatient of the whole farce. Why keep him here like this? Why go through all the empty formality of a trial? Why not just set him against a wall facing a firing squad and give him swift and final peace?

He moved again, sweating, narrowing his eyes so that the shimmering sunlight reflected on the ceiling broke into a thousand shards of splintered brilliance, each shard winking and flickering with hypnotic insistence.

Remember! Remember! Remember!

'No!' he gasped. 'No!'

You will remember, flickered the sunlight. *Listen and obey. You will remember everything. Everything!*

He shuddered as, from somewhere in the deep recesses of his mind, he heard the echoing screams of dying men.

Remember!

Rolling from the bunk, he stood, shuddering, sweat beading his forehead to run over his face. Toilet facilities stood in the corner of the cell. He twisted the faucet, filled the bowl, ducked his head into the water and drenched hair and neck. The water was tepid but it helped. Rising, he shook droplets from his hair, ducked again, kept his face below the surface until his lungs ached from the lack of air.

Remember, he thought. Remember what? Mentally he searched the blank spot in his memory but found nothing.

Then why had he heard the screams of dying men? A dream, he told himself. That's all it was. A dream. A nightmare that somehow got itself mixed up with something I can't remember. But why can't I remember?

He ducked his face again and pulled the lever and watched as the water ran from the bowl. It vanished with a liquid gurgle. Memories, he thought, all gone down the drain like that water. But who pulled the lever on me?

He turned as sounds came from beyond the cell door.

The soft pad of footsteps, a metallic jingle as of keys, a definite click as the lock was operated. The door opened, allowed a man to pass through, closed again.

Carmodine blinked. 'You!'

'So you remember me? That is good.' Doctor Paul Brensco stepped closer, walking as a fencer walks, delicately, poised on the balls of his feet and ready to jump at any second.

He was blond, impeccably dressed and with eyes of intense blue. A thin moustache accentuated the sardonic lines of his mouth. He was tall but appeared even taller because of his slimness but there was nothing weak about him; like a rapier he was built for economical strength.

Paul Brensco, scientist-adventurer, Carmodine's one-time rival.

But not now, he thought tiredly. All that is over. Now he's the kingpin and he's way out ahead in a class of his own. Aloud he said, 'Have you come to gloat, Paul?'

Brensco shook his head. 'No, Jules. Have I anything to gloat about?'

'I should think you have.' Carmodine sat on the edge of a cot, leaving the stool for his visitor. 'Or aren't you human enough to enjoy the sweet taste of victory?'

'All that is past,' said Brensco evenly. 'Once, I admit, I hated you. At the Academy when you, with your great, ox-like body, used to be first in athletics, I swore that one day I would best you. Later, when you were given the command of that exploration vessel to Pluto, I could have killed you and enjoyed doing it. But you were a man then. Now . . . ' He shrugged and made no attempt to disguise his contempt. 'Crater 4,' he mused. 'Mutants, scum, degenerates killing themselves with narcotics, but they have a reason. They were born to suffer. But you? Did you have to join them?'

Carmodine made no answer.

'You've proved that you are weak,' continued Brensco. 'A man who ran away, who tried to escape into the dream-world of drugs, who mingled with the mutants as if they were his brothers.' He paused. 'Brothers and sisters,' he said meaningfully. 'Things with too many arms or no arms at all. Creatures with scales instead of skin. Freaks, monsters, hellspawn! And you joined them!'

'Why don't you spit if you feel like it?' Carmodine spoke without emotion but inwardly he was fighting the automatic tension, the readiness for combat that Brensco could always induce. Like cat and dog, he thought. We have a natural antipathy. A glandular reaction that spawns automatic violence. He forced himself to relax. Now there was no longer any need to fight. 'Go ahead,' he invited. 'I won't mind. I don't care what you do or what you call me. What any man calls me. It doesn't matter any more.' He smiled without humour. 'A dead man is beyond injury.'

'You consider yourself dead?'

'What else? I deserted my command and that is a capital charge. I crashed my ship and failed to report and they could execute me for that alone. I'm dead, Paul. In a little while, I'll be cremated. It's just a matter of taking care of the formalities. So why don't you get the hell out of here and leave me alone!'

He'd been shouting, but it didn't matter. The smooth plastic lining walls, floor and ceiling absorbed the sound. Only Brensco could have heard and that didn't matter either. Nothing mattered. It was, as he had said, only a matter of taking care of the formalities. Now, if the other man would leave him alone, he could perhaps get some sleep. There was an escape in sleep . . . if he did not dream.

Brensco looked down at the stool, hooked it towards him, deliberately sat down. 'Why?' he demanded.

'I'm tired. I . . .'

'I'm not talking about you asking me to leave,' interrupted Brensco. 'Why do it? Desert your command, I mean. Crash your ship and run. Why, Jules? Damn you, man! Why?'

Carmodine shrugged. 'That's my business.'

'No it isn't, Jules,' corrected Brensco. 'Not any longer.' He paused and added, quietly, 'The Homogenetic League has organized a second expedition. I have been given the command.'

Carmodine drew a deep breath. 'To Pluto?'

'Yes.'

'Is there any point in my warning you against taking that command?'

'None at all.'

'I thought not,' said Carmodine. 'So?'

Brensco leaned forward, one elbow resting on his knee to support his weight, eyes like blue spears of ice as they probed Carmodine's own. Blue against jet as it had been so often in the past. 'I want to know what happened to you out there, Jules,' he said evenly. 'What happened to the men with you. I've got to know.'

Carmodine leaned back against the wall of his cell and looked at the ceiling. On the plastic reflected sunshine danced in shimmering patterns from the broad moat surrounding the jail. If he narrowed his eyes and squinted, the patterns would splinter into flickering shards and each shard would have an insistent voice.

'Please, Jules.'

Carmodine lowered his eyes. 'You're begging,' he said wonderingly. 'You.' And then added, 'I can't tell you, Paul. Surely you must know that?'

'No, Jules. I think you can tell me if you really wanted. If you weren't so much a coward.'

'Damn you!' said Carmodine, bridling. 'Go to hell!'

Brensco refused to show his annoyance. 'It is you who will be going to hell unless you agree to cooperate,' he said. 'Must I remind you that all persons convicted and sentenced to execution could be handed over to the Federation laboratories for experimental surgery? Few are, but, in your case, there is no doubt. The crime was too great. The wilful refusal to merit consideration by withholding information is too heinous an act for any consideration of mercy. You are going to suffer, Jules. More than you can possibly imagine. Unless . . . ' His pause held a world of meaning.

Carmodine sighed. 'You're wasting your time, Paul. And let me put you straight on one thing. No matter how they intend to kill me that is the worst they can do. The very worst. Death is no hell. Hell is where you're going. It's waiting for you on Pluto and believe me, Paul, you're welcome to every little bit of it.'

He shivered and wondered why. I'm like a child, he thought. The very mention of Pluto is enough to trigger a reactionary fear-response. But why? What happened to make me so terrified?

Abruptly he rose and crossed to the bowl. He filled it with water and doused his head again, holding his breath until his lungs ached, wondering if a man could deliberately drown himself in such a manner.

Brensco watched him, making no comment until Carmodine returned to the bunk. 'You mean it,' he said.

'This isn't an act. You honestly believe there is something terrible out there.' He rested his hand on Carmodine's arm, dug steel fingers into the flesh. 'Tell me,' he demanded. 'Talk, damn you! Talk, or I'll sear your brain with the psychoprobe!'

'Again?' Carmodine laughed at Brensco's expression. 'I know you too well, Paul.

You wouldn't waste time like this without a good reason. You've tried the probes and they didn't work. Correct?'

'You were raving,' Brensco said sullenly. 'The probes were the quickest way to restore your mental stability but, in achieving it, we drove the thing which had made you insane too deep. We couldn't surface it and still keep you alive. Somehow you had built a fantastically strong defence mechanism. The psyche was determined that you should suffer physical death rather than total recall.'

Brensco looked thoughtfully at the man on the cot. 'A problem,' he said musingly. 'One that I could solve, given time. There are other techniques, slower, but safe and infallible. Given time, it would be possible for me to force you to achieve total recall. Make you remember every detail of your conscious and unconscious life from the moment of conception. But I cannot use those techniques. Need I say how unfortunate the inability is?'

'It seems,' said Carmodine dryly, 'that a prisoner has some rights. Any surgery performed on me will be by the

Federation, not by you.'

'Exactly. So I am appealing to you, Jules.' Brensco's eyes were level, direct. 'To ensure against the failure of my expedition, I must know what happened to you. Did the crew mutiny?'

'No.'

'How can you be sure? If you can't remember, then how can you be certain?'

'I'm certain.'

'But . . . '

Carmodine shook his head, refusing to listen. How could he make this selfishly cold-blooded scientist understand? How could any man know what it was like out there, way beyond Saturn, way past any hope of rescue where the stars began to look like watching eyes and space itself crouched like a black velvet tiger eager for blood and brain and bone? The crew hadn't mutinied. They had all been too close for that. They had been like brothers and he had betrayed them.

Why had he thought of that?

Brensco was patient. 'Was it the engines?'

'No.'

15

'What, then? Radiation sickness? Dormant allergies? Mental unrest? Tell me, Jules. What was it?'

'Hell,' said Carmodine quietly. 'It could have been nothing less.' He squeezed shut his eyes and spoke from the safety of darkness. 'I'd tell you if I could, Paul. Our rivalry is over. What difference could anything make now? Believe me, I simply can't remember. If I could, then, as you've told me, I'd be suicidally insane. The knowledge would kill me.'

'Lack of it could do more,' snapped Brensco, his patience exhausted. 'Remember what I told you? The experimental laboratories won't be gentle. They will remove the brain from your skull and torment it for a dozen years. Don't be a fool. Talk while you've got the chance!'

Carmodine opened his eyes and studied the ceiling.

'Again that old threat? How often must I tell you that I am not afraid to die?'

Brensco rose from the stool and looked down at the prisoner. 'No,' he said thickly. 'Death is too easy. There is always death. Many think you should die. There is the matter of a ship destroyed, five men missing, a man who had to be dragged from Crater 4. By all the laws of space and the Federation you merit death. But you can be killed at any time.'

Carmodine frowned. 'What do you mean?'

'Within your skull lies knowledge which will be lost if you die. Information that cost billions to obtain, data that took the lives of five men, facts essential to the safety of the second expedition. My expedition.' Brensco paused, his blue-eyed face as hard as if carved from stone. 'I do not intend that it shall fail. Therefore I am going to get the knowledge I need.'

Fear tightened Carmodine's stomach. The reactive fear of the unknown. 'How?'

'It is really quite simple.' Brensco relaxed, a man supremely confident of himself and his capabilities. He turned to the cell door, knocked, waited until the guard outside had tripped the lock. He swung open the panel and hesitated with it half open. 'The Homogenetic League is not without influence,' he said. 'I should hardly have to remind you of that. The Federation is agreeable to certain suggestions that have been made. I am taking you with me, Jules. Back to Pluto with the second expedition.'

He slammed the door in Carmodine's face.

2

Illraya

On the plain, the ship rose proudly towards the sky, brilliant sunshine clothing the sleek lines in shimmers of reflected glory, the burnished plates catching and accentuating the glare. Carmodine examined it as the heliojet swung in a wide circle towards a landing at the edge of the field. It was, he guessed, a modified ore transport from the Belt, the capacious interior converted to hold extra fuel and provisions for the long journey.

The heliojet pilot noted Carmodine's interest. 'You know something about ships, mister?'

'A little,' said Carmodine dryly.

'That one's special,' volunteered the pilot. 'They've been working on it for a long time, and at top pressure all the way. Conversion work mostly. Extra engines, strengthening the hull, stuff like that. They've even fitted weapon turrets and launchers for atomic missiles. What the hell do they expect to find out there?'

He didn't wait for an answer. 'Pluto,' he said. 'Right on the edge of the Big Dark. It makes you cold just to think about it. What'll happen if anything goes wrong? Suppose they get hit by something? There'll be no chance of rescue. Nothing.' He scowled at his controls. 'I was talking to the wife about it. You know what she said? She said that anyone who goes in that crate has more guts than sense. Me? I wouldn't go if they offered me a fortune.'

'Sure,' said one of the two guards. 'A guy must have a hole in the head to go on a trip like that. How close can you set us down?'

'Two hundred be close enough?'

'In this heat?' The second guard was a plump, sweating man with lobeless ears. 'Why can't you drop down right smack on the ramp?'

'Two hundred yards,' insisted the pilot stubbornly. 'That's my limit.'

Carmodine watched as the ground came up to meet them. Ships now had clean exhausts and there could be no more Craters, but old fears clung against all reason. The plump guard turned as they left the cabin.

'Wait for us,' he ordered. 'We won't be long.' He jerked the chain that connected his wrist to Carmodine's. 'Let's get this over with.'

The pilot had landed almost in the shadow of the vessel so that Carmodine could see it against the blue of the sky as a graceful silhouette, the upper part flashing with reflected light. The sight triggered old memories. There had been youth and friends and the prospect of high adventure. There had been ambition and pride and the sense of achievement. For a moment, he felt the old emotions and then tasted bitterness as he remembered. This was not his ship. His command lay in scattered ruin in the Mato Grosso. His crew . . .

He didn't want to think about his crew.

He stumbled, almost falling, feeling the spiteful jerk of the chain on the manacle locked around his wrist. His foot kicked metal and he realized they had reached the foot of the ramp. Brensco leaned from the open port, looking down with a thin, supercilious smile.

'Welcome to my command, Jules,' he said clearly. 'Are you ready to come aboard?'

'Have I any choice?'

'None at all. But you have a choice about how you board. You can walk or be carried. Which is it to be?'

Silently Carmodine held out his wrist for the plump guard to unlock the manacle. The metal had chafed his wrist. Absently he rubbed the sore place as he climbed the ramp. At the entrance to the port, he turned and looked over the sun-drenched plain. Heat made the buildings shimmer, the tiny figures of watching people somehow unreal. He felt someone standing close beside him.

'It's a long way down,' said Brensco. 'If you dived and landed head-first, you'd probably smash your skull.'

'You try it,' suggested Carmodine. 'I'll stand by to cheer.'

A hand gripped his shoulder, jerked, spun him from the mouth of the open port into the vestibule. Brensco stood before the opening, dark against the sunlight, legs straddled and rigid with tension. 'Let's get one thing clear,' he said coldly. 'This is my ship and you're under my jurisdiction. One wrong move and I'll put you in chains for the whole voyage. Do you understand?'

'You're the captain,' agreed Carmodine thickly. He felt the familiar strain, the release of adrenalin into his bloodstream as his body readied itself for action. 'You wear the braid and give the orders, but don't kid yourself that it makes you a man. Touch me again, you motherless scum, and I'll tear you apart!'

He ducked as a fist drove towards his mouth. The first blow missed, the second cut a gash over one eye, the third jarred against the muscles of his stomach. Weaving, Carmodine blocked the attack and slammed a fist to Brensco's jaw with a punch to the heart and then aimed for the spot between the eyes.

He missed.

Brensco was a trained athlete, a fencer with all a swordsman's quickness and in perfect condition. His own fist crashed against Carmodine's mouth as his knee lifted viciously towards the groin.

Carmodine twisted, spat a mouthful of blood and like a released spring, leapt forward.

A guard caught his arm. Another sprang between Carmodine and Brensco. A third grabbed his other arm and dragged him backwards. Two others stood by, thick clubs poised in their hands. One of them spoke to Brensco.

'Your orders, sir? Shall we put him in irons?'

Brensco touched his jaw, his nose, looked at the red stain on his fingers as if he couldn't believe he saw his own blood.

'Sir?'

'Yes,' said Brensco. 'That is . . . no. I — ' He broke off as a woman came from the inner entrance of the vestibule. 'Never mind. He won't cause any more trouble. You may go.' He waited until the guards had left and then said, 'Illraya, allow me to introduce you to your patient. This is

Jules Carmodine. Carmodine, this is Doctor Illraya Semorova of the University of Curitiba. She is coming with us to Pluto.'

Carmodine made no comment.

'Illraya will work on you during the journey,' said Brensco. 'I want the information you hold as soon as possible. Naturally you will cooperate. If you do not, I shall take steps to persuade you. A current of electricity applied directly to the nervous system, for example. Or an induced drug addiction and the later withholding of supplies. There are many ways.' He glanced at the instrument on his wrist. 'We must prepare for take-off. I suggest you both get immediately to work.'

On the way from the vestibule, Carmodine had the opportunity to study the woman. She was tall, with sea-green eyes spaced widely on a face which held vague hints of Mongolian ancestors. Her skin was a golden cream. The figure beneath the regulation space garb of high-collared blouse, pants and knee-high boots was rounded with the full curves of maturity. A mane of burnished copper hair fell to her shoulders, held in place by a fillet of gold. She felt the impact of his eyes and turned, smiling.

'You approve?'

'Of you as a woman? Very much. Of you as a shipmate? No.'

'You think that my place is on the ground?' The smile grew wider. 'In a kitchen, perhaps? Keeping home for some man? Nursing babies?'

He returned her smile. 'There are worse things a woman could do, but I didn't mean that. This journey isn't going to be a pleasure trip. I don't think there is a place for a woman aboard. Any woman.'

'We are not always the arbiters of our fate,' she said enigmatically. 'Incidentally, Captain Brensco made a slight error in our introduction. He said that I was going to work on you. That is wrong. I hope to work with you. I am sure you appreciate the difference.' She paused before a door, opened it, gestured for him to pass inside. 'Have you known each other long?'

'Almost thirty years,' said Carmodine.

The cabin was spacious and contained

a therapy couch, together with a mass of scientific apparatus. Illraya sank into a chair, gestured for him to take another.

'Since you were together at the orphanage,' she said, 'would you like to tell me about it?'

'You know?'

'I've done my homework. Your early lives are a matter of record. You don't like each other, do you?'

'No,' he admitted. 'We never have. Even as kids we were rivals. Something made us want to beat each other all the time. At sport, at work, at examinations, even in the social life, what we had of it. Maybe that rivalry was the best thing that could have happened to us. It made us work. We took our science doctorates together. We graduated at the same time. But it made no difference. We still don't like each other.'

'A mutual antipathy,' she murmured. 'A common phenomenon but, in your case, unusually well-developed.'

'We seemed to break even,' he continued. 'He was the better dancer, I the better swimmer. He the better fencer, I the better runner. Things like that. When we graduated, we both went to work for the Homogenetic League. Brensco turned towards the research side of things while I entered the exploratory field. When the first Pluto expedition came up, it was a battle between us as to who should get the command. I had the experience, so it fell to me. Now it's Paul's turn.'

She nodded. 'I see. And that fight you had? The one in the vestibule. Was that over anything special?'

'I stepped out of line,' he admitted. 'I called him something I shouldn't have. I mentioned his mother.' He met her uncompromising stare. 'We were both orphans, as you know, with both parents dead. At the Academy, they used to taunt us by claiming that we were androids, that we had never had any parents at all. It was a joke, of course — you know what kids are like — but Brensco always took it very seriously.'

'And you?'

'I learned early that a man has to be able to laugh at himself before he can claim the right to laugh at others.'

'A good thing to learn,' she said. 'Is there anything else you want to tell me?'

He didn't answer and she frowned at his silence. 'You have no cause to be reticent. My position in this is very simple. Paul tells me that you have information that is vital to the success of this expedition. With your help, I will obtain that information. But you must trust me, have confidence in me, believe that I want to help you.'

He leaned back, admiring the colour of her hair. 'You know, of course, that I am a deserter? A man who has merited death?'

'I am not interested in that.'

'Not even as relative information?'

'In that respect only, but it isn't really important.' She leaned towards him and he caught the odour of her hair, the clean washed scent of her skin. 'Your sufferings in the past have robbed you of a great deal of vitality. I intend to restore it. To do that, I must have your full trust and cooperation. Only then can we hope to clear the mental blockages cluttering your mind. Memory must be regained in total recall.'

'I'm not sure that I like what you're getting at,' said Carmodine slowly. 'Brensco used something like that as a threat. Total recall. Is that what you're after?'

'It is the best way.'

'Best for whom? Me?'

Her eyes were direct. 'Yes.'

'I wonder.' Leaning forward, he took her hand. It was slim, delicately formed, fragile against his own strength.

'Whatever it was I've forgotten had the power to send me insane. That is why I've forgotten it. Or so Paul explained. You can surely see why I am reluctant to agree with what you say.'

A man ran past the door down the corridor outside. A low hum echoed through the ship and an emotionless voice came from a speaker in one corner of the room. 'Ship readying for take-off. Hull sealed. All personnel at stations.'

Illraya ignored the voice. 'You believe that if you remember your past, you will automatically go insane?'

'So I've been told.'

'That won't happen, you know. With your help, we shall revive an incident. At first it will be bad, but then, as you go over and over the occurrence, the destructive charge will dissipate. The incident will no longer hold emotional dangers and have no more meaning than a tale told by another over a glass of wine.'

'You would like me to believe that,' he said.

'Yes,' she admitted. 'I would very much like you to believe it because it is the truth. Normal psychiatric treatment. I've used it a thousand times in one form or another. You know, Jules,' she said, 'the human brain is a peculiar device. In a sense it is our only contact with the universe. We must believe what our senses tell us because we have no way of disproving them. And yet, we know they are lying. Our eyes, for example. We see everything upside-down and our brain reverses the image so that we can understand it. How could you ever persuade anyone of that? Without scientific proof, the thing is so obviously wrong. Yet it is a proven fact.

'And it is the same with you. You are

31

convinced that a certain result will bring a certain reaction. You have equated remembrance with insanity and now tend to think of one as being equal to the other. Remembrance equals insanity, so insanity equals remembrance. Wrong, Jules! So terribly wrong!'

He smiled at her intensity. 'All right,' he said, 'I believe you.'

'You must!' She looked at him and then added quietly, 'Why do you hate yourself?'

The total unexpectedness of the question threw him momentarily off balance. The reaction was swift, the automatic denial of something so transparently false, and then the slow acceptance of the unpalatable fact that the woman could be right.

'Deep inside yourself is the desire to be punished,' said Illraya seriously. 'I am not talking of the death-wish, but something more personal, something laid on and over the universal yearning to die. The way you lived in Crater 4 wasn't the act of a man seeking death. Death was too simple, too easy. First you had to be punished and who better to do it than yourself? Punishing the man you hated. Hurting yourself because you judged that you deserved pain. That fight in the vestibule — did you insult the captain because you wanted to feel the weight of his anger? Are you disappointed that you are not in chains?'

He smiled. 'Hardly. If I were, I wouldn't be enjoying such delightful company.'

'Careful, Jules,' she warned. 'Don't enjoy it too much. A man who hates himself cannot permit the man he hates too much pleasure. He will find ways to stop it. Attempted murder, for example, or, more likely, attempted rape.'

'Attempted? Are you so certain it will only be that?'

'Very certain. I have faced this before Jules. I am not untrained in the means of self-protection.' She rose smiling. 'Some wine?'

It was from the Grosso, tart and clean to the tongue. He savoured it as she resumed her seat.

'Well, Jules? Do you know why you hate yourself?'

'No.'

'A pity. But then, if you knew, there would be no need of therapy.' She sipped at her glass, the golden wine more golden against her cheek. 'The area of your amnesia is interesting,' she continued. 'We shall have to plot its exact duration. But that can wait for later. Now let us drink wine together and try a little experiment. Why do you hate yourself?'

'I told you, I . . . '

'Why do you hate yourself?'

With an effort, he restrained his anger. 'I don't know. If I do, and I'm taking your word for it, I can't guess the reason.'

Slowly she drank, eyes greenly levelled over the rim of her glass and, the glass empty, she refilled it from the bottle.

'You are a coward,' she said flatly. 'You are afraid to face the truth.' And then. sharply, 'Why do you hate yourself?'

The stem of the glass snapped in his hand.

'Coward! Why do you hate yourself?'

'Shut your mouth, you scheming bitch!' Glass shattered as he flung aside the broken fragments. 'What the hell do you want me to say? I don't know, I tell you. If I ever did know, I've forgotten and I don't want to remember. Damn you, woman! Something's waiting out there on Pluto and I'd rather die than have to face it again.'

'Is that why you can't remember?'

'Yes. Yes, damn you! What else could it be?'

Her face grew hard, the cheekbones prominent beneath the satin skin. 'You're lying, Jules. That isn't the reason and you know it. Have the guts to face up to the truth. Don't be a coward.'

Anger sent blood racing in his ears. How dare the bitch call him that?

'Think!' she insisted. 'Don't run away from it. Have the courage to stare it in the face. What reasons has a man for hating himself? Fear? Shame? Guilt? Because he is a traitor? Because he is a coward? Because he is a liar? Tell me Jules. Tell me!'

He stared at her, almost afraid of the wide, green eyes that could probe so deep and learn so much. Why did she have to keep hurting him? Why couldn't she just leave him alone?

The voice from the speaker broke the silence. 'Warning. Take positions for take-off. Blasting in one minute. Siren will sound at thirty seconds. Prepare for take-off.'

Carmodine forced himself to relax. In this vessel, he was just a passenger. Others had the essential duties, but it was hard not to go through them in his mind.

The contact with the external buildings, the check on instruments, the telltales from the engine rooms, the hydroponic chamber, the compensators and the myriad devices perfected so as to enable men to survive in the void.

Brensco would be in the captain's chair. His crew would be in almost physical touch. Above waited space and the great emptiness where stars and planets swam like motes of dust. The asteroids, the outer planets, Pluto!

Carmodine swallowed, perspiration breaking out on his forehead as his mind skirted the edges of what-he-must-not-remember. Again he heard the thin screams of dying men, saw their faces, the familiar shapes of old friends. Don and Joe, Sam and

Chandra, old Evans who tended the engines and who was always good for a song or yarn to while away the boredom between planetfalls.

Good men. True, loyal, faithful and brave. They had trusted him to take them to the edge of the Big Dark. Followed him out to where the sun was just another star. They had trusted him and he . . .

What had he done?

He straightened, blinking, his mind a swirling mass of coloured smoke. Red and grey and smooth, rich brown, burnished copper and the wash of sea-green waters. Hard, blue, like chipped sapphires and twinkling somethings which could have been diamonds or stars.

Diamonds on the soft black velvet of space.

From somewhere down an endless tunnel, he heard the harsh call of a siren.

They were about to leave! Ready to head up and out and away! To go back to Pluto! To go back! Back!

'Jules!'

He heard the cry, faint, distant, felt the slap of a hand as if it were a feather, saw the sea-green pools of her eyes as she tried to read his soul.

'Jules! Don't!'

The woman was a witch. She would tear him apart and laugh at what she found. The eyes again. Wide. Green. Calculating.

'The psychic trauma is incredibly strong,' she said as if to an invisible audience. 'A strong personality . . . defeat the whole object . . . sedation . . . quickly, before . . . '

A pungent smell and a cloud of blackness that rose and grew and filled the entire universe with nighted oblivion.

3

Mutiny

They had more than three billion miles to go and before they had covered a third of it, Carmodine knew there would be trouble.

Not from the ship. The Homogenetic League engineers had chosen well and had taken care over the conversion. The big cargo boat stood the strain of the added thrust of extra engines, the balance was good so that the course was true. The great venturis were silent now, the ship coasting towards the edge of the system, the solar drag gradually robbing them of momentum. The ship was operating with maximum efficiency. The life-support apparatus was satisfactory.

Yet trouble was inevitable.

'The fool doesn't know how to handle men,' said Carmodine bitterly. He stretched on the therapy couch and glowered at the ceiling. 'He's buying bad trouble every time he opens his mouth.'

Illraya adjusted a mechanism. 'Brensco?'

'Who else?' Carmodine lifted himself on one elbow.

'You can smell the stink of it as you walk through the ship. Frustration. Hate, hurt pride. It's all over the place.'

Glowering, he sank back on the couch. His hands clenched as he thought of the captain. In space, men could not be treated as if they were unfeeling machines. The emptiness was too big, their reliance on each other too great. And it was more than that. They were in a hostile environment, which held a strange and terrible beauty. The cold, harsh indifference of the void made men feel overly sensitive. Their pride became inflated by the necessity of personal identification. They had to be recognized as individuals, not machines, not factors in an equation. In space, a man demanded that he be treated for what he was.

'He's doing things the hard way,' he told Illraya. 'Brensco must think he's back on Earth with an army behind him to back his orders. Surely you must have noticed it.'

'No,' she said. 'I haven't. But this is my first time in space. I don't know how men should act out here. Tell me.'

Carmodine frowned. 'It's plain enough. A man is a man. Forget that fact and you turn him into something else. Maybe a machine, a robot of flesh and blood and no brain. The old foot soldiers were like that — conditioned so they could only react to orders and unable to use their own intelligence. They were made to run into enemy fire, actually attack machine-guns as if they hoped to swamp the guns with targets. Or you could make him turn the other way, insult him just that once too often. Then he's got to stand up for himself, prove he's a man and not a thing to be kicked aside. In space, we don't make men into robots. We daren't.'

'What you are saying,' said Illraya thoughtfully, 'is that there could be a mutiny. Is that it?'

Carmodine nodded.

'But such things are rare,' she protested. 'I've never heard of men doing

41

that since we reached the asteroids.'

'The last mutiny in space was eighty-three years ago,' said Carmodine. 'The ship was an exploratory vessel of the Federation. It was ordered to find Vulcan — or rather to determine once and for all whether such a planet exists. The captain made the mistake of treating his men as if they were unthinking morons. When they realized they were past the orbit of Mercury and heading directly towards the Sun, they forced a meeting. The captain ordered them back to their posts and threatened to shoot the first man who disobeyed.'

Illraya was interested. 'And . . . ?'

'He managed to kill two men. The rest took him, put him in a spacesuit and evicted him through the airlock. Then they headed for Earth and trial. Can you guess the verdict?'

'Guilty?'

'Of course. The survivors were condemned to execution. When the news got out, every space man stationed on Earth refused to board a vessel. The Luna Station joined the strike. It lasted three weeks and, at the end of it, the men were reprieved. The Federation lost power it has never regained and no space man now can be regarded as an unfeeling robot useful to take orders and nothing else.'

'Interesting. The Homogenetic League must have been founded about then.' Illraya shrugged. 'They should have made it a law that each ship should carry a qualified psychologist.'

'There's no need,' said Carmodine. 'Captains are trained in elementary psychology. But out here it's the old problem. Who is going to watch the watcher? You?'

'I'll talk to him if I have to,' said Illraya. 'But what can I say? I've no experience with conditions out here. You have.'

Carmodine frowned. 'Are you saying that I should help Brensco?'

'Why not?' She smiled and wheeled the machine she had been adjusting back into its rack. 'Look at it this way,' she suggested. 'You aren't helping him, you're helping every other man in the ship besides yourself.'

Put that way, he couldn't refuse.

Illraya's therapy room was down towards the lower part of the vessel, close to the storage compartments and hydroponic tanks. Brensco was in officer-country, high towards the nose, where he could stand before the screens and look at the star-flecked night of space. A guard halted Carmodine as he entered the passage leading to the control room.

'Sorry, mister. No one is permitted down here.'

'I want to talk to the captain,' said Carmodine patiently. 'Please inform him of that fact.'

'What's your business? Is it important?' The guard hesitated. 'He'll ask,' he said. 'He doesn't want to be disturbed for trifles. Maybe you'd better wait the routine inspection and grab him as he goes past.'

'Maybe you'd better carry my message,' said Carmodine bleakly. 'Jump to it, mister!'

'Yes, sir!' Then the guard realized who had snapped the command. 'Hey! Who the hell are you to . . . ' He gave a disgusted snort. 'Never mind. Just wait here and I'll see if the captain is interested in what you have to say.'

He vanished down the passage and returned wearing a wide grin. 'What did I tell you, mister? No soap. Like I told you before, your best chance is to grab him while he's on routine inspection.'

'When will that be?'

'Another hour,' said the guard. 'Maybe longer. Who can tell?'

It was three hours before Brensco decided to make inspection of the ship. Attended by guards, he swung down the passage, cold eyes glinting as Carmodine stepped forward. He made no effort to halt.

'Captain!' Carmodine put out his hand and caught Brensco's sleeve. 'This is important, Paul. I've got to talk to you.'

'Is it about Pluto?'

'No. About the ship. I think you should know that things are . . . ' He broke off as Brensco pulled away. 'Paul! This concerns your command!'

Brensco halted and turned, his thin-lipped face a cruel mask. 'I'll give you one warning,' he said. 'Shout at me like that again and I'll have you flogged until the flesh peels from your bones. I want only one thing from you, Carmodine. The knowledge inside your head. Anything else you may have to say is of no interest to me. Especially anything you have to say about my ship. My ship, Carmodine. I suggest you remember that.'

He stalked down the passage, arrogantly proud, and Carmodine felt his spine crawl as he stared after him. Something had happened to the cold-blooded scientist. Long hours of lonely contemplation of the universe had worked its devilment. Brensco had made the mistake of isolating himself from his men. Not for him the yarns and songs and warmth of friendship.

Now he walked like a king among slaves.

'Paranoia,' said Illraya when he told her about it. 'Delusions of grandeur. He'll be suspicious, afraid that you might want to take his position. My advice is for you to keep well out of his way.'

'And let the mutiny take place?'

'If there is a mutiny,' she said. 'You could be wrong, Jules. Your opinion could be influenced by personal feelings.'

'I don't like Paul, so I hope something bad will happen to him?' Carmodinc looked thoughtful. 'And what worse than a mutiny could hit a ship's captain? You think that's it?'

Illraya turned from where she stood by her therapeutic machines. 'Is a possibility,' she said.

Brooding, he thought about it. Was he jealous? Reading into trifling detail what he wanted to find? Did he just envy Brensco for the command he had? Lying back on the therapy couch, he assessed his data. The ship was clean and perhaps a little too clean. Made-up work was always dangerous. Men obeyed orders, but with an exaggerated speed. He had heard little laughter and no good-natured grumbling. And against that, it was a much larger vessel than the one he had commanded on the first expedition. The complement was greater. It wouldn't be possible for Brensco to have the same intimacy with his men as Carmodine had done, even if Brensco had wanted to.

And yet could he be so mistaken?

'A week,' he said aloud. 'Unless Paul changes his ways he'll have a mutiny on his hands within a week.' He looked at Illraya's startled face. 'I'm hoping I'm wrong,' he said. 'I want to be wrong. But I don't think I am. Maybe you should tell him.'

'Why?' She came and sat beside him on the couch. Looking up, he could see her profile, the high cheekbones and full curve of her lips. Light from the glowtubes glowed from the copper of her hair. 'Let's forget Paul for now. Tell me more about yourself. About some of the men you shipped with. Your first command. The expeditions you were on. Things you did and saw.'

'The last expedition?'

'If you wish. Why was it launched in the first place? Trade?'

He nodded. 'The Homogenetic League is looking towards the future. Other than a few of the moons of Jupiter and Saturn, there are no habitable worlds beyond the Belt. Uranus is barely possible, but the League decided to go for broke. Pluto has about the same diameter as Luna and about half the mass of Earth. As a cold laboratory, it couldn't be better. The temperature must be close to absolute zero. But there's a more important reason than any of those. When other minor bodies were discovered beyond Pluto, and that Pluto itself had a moon, it was thought at first that Pluto must have been the innermost minor planet, part of a mass of early material in the solar system that never made it to become real planets.'

'The Kuiper Belt and the Oort Cloud?'

'Yes. But in more recent years a lot of scientists think that maybe Pluto itself doesn't really belong to our solar system. They think that it could have come drifting in from the Big Dark, a wanderer from some stellar catastrophe. In that case, think of the rewards that might be waiting to be picked up.'

'New isotopes,' she said thoughtfully. 'Perhaps even seeds, spores and spawn. Alien life. Truly alien. Based on a different life cycle from anything we know.' Excitement warmed her cheeks. 'The few things we've found so far are linked by the common elements of the Sun — bacteria on Mars, some crystals from Mercury. Nothing we could begin to think of as intelligent life. Distorted species of similar growths to be found on Earth.'

'The Belt is nothing but shattered rock,' he said as she paused. 'Metals and a few unusual alloys. If the planet that made the asteroids — if it ever was a planet — ever had life, we haven't found signs of it. Which leaves only the satellites of Jupiter and Saturn, and they are from the parent body. Nothing alien about those.'

'So that leaves Pluto.' Illraya shrugged. 'Well, we'll find out all about it when we get there.' He caught the watchful glance of her eyes. 'You're getting better,' she commented. 'We can actually talk about the place without you displaying withdrawal symptoms.'

'Maybe. But I still don't like to talk about it.'

'Then we'll talk about something else.

When was the first time you went into space?'

'Quite a few years ago,' he said dryly. 'And the only thing that happened was that I got sick.' He joined her smile, then sobered. 'There was a time,' he said slowly, 'not too many years ago now . . . it was on the third or maybe fourth trip to the Red Spot. You know it?'

'On Jupiter. Yes.'

'We didn't land, of course. There was no hope of that, the gravity well is too deep. We hung on the jets and took atmosphere samples. It was a little tricky. The wind was thin but strong and it was a matter of balance. Well, we took the samples and everything was going along fine until we got caught by an eddy current. It was a twisting mass of methane and ammonia in a thousand-mile-per-hour wind. I was young, inexperienced, and it caught me by surprise. Alone, I wouldn't have stood a chance.'

'What happened? Tell me all of it,' she insisted. 'Everything.'

He grew tense as he related the incident, describing the insane fury of the wind, the relentless pull of a gravity close to three times normal, the electric haloes and shocking fire-balls, the pain of static current. He painted the scene in vivid colours, feeling again the tension and despair, the sick knowledge of utter helplessness and the crazed search for a way to stay alive.

'I was lucky,' he said. 'I had a new engineer. An oldtimer who had magic in his fingers. Evans, his name was. Evans?'

He frowned and absently touched his forehead. His fingers came away wet with perspiration. He looked at the film of moisture and shuddered.

'That name,' said Illraya softly. 'The engineer who saved your life. What was his name?'

'Evans,' he muttered. 'Evans.'

'He went with you to Pluto,' she said casually. 'Tell me more, Jules.'

'No,' he said. He looked at his hands. They were trembling. 'No,' he said again. 'I'm not a thing for you to prod and manipulate like a specimen on a slab.' He swung his legs over the edge of the couch and sat upright. He turned to stare into the woman's face. 'Listen,' he said. 'Therapy is one thing. I can't stop you from doing what you want at those times. But this wasn't therapy. You got me talking, remembering . . . ' He broke off. 'Is that the way you play?'

'This is no game, Jules.' Her eyes met his own, hard, green, penetrating. 'It never was and it's getting more serious every day. Don't you understand that this vessel and the lives of all of us could depend on you? I wasn't trying to trick you! I mean you well. You must believe that.'

'Does it matter what I believe?' He found tissues and wiped his face. 'Never mind,' he said as he threw the wad into a disposal chute. 'What's done is done. The past is dead. Forget it.'

'Not when it affects the living!' Her hands were unexpectedly strong as she gripped his shoulders and spun him to face her. 'Look at you! A man who should be full of life. A man with everything to live for, and yet you act like a man without a soul. If the dead have the power to do that to the living, then we must obliterate the dead. They were your friends, these men you refuse to remember. Tell me, Jules would they want to see you as you are? Or would they rather you be as they they knew you . . . big and strong and worthy of their loyalty?'

'Loyalty!' He twisted from her grasp, rose and paced the floor of the cabin. His boots made soft, padding sounds. The noise was too quiet. He needed something to drown the thin screams of dying men. 'You don't know what you're saying,' he flung at her. 'You're guessing. What would those men want with me now?'

'They were your friends.'

'Once, perhaps,' he admitted. 'Now they're buried. Like my memories. Let them stay that way.' He halted, glowering at the woman where she sat on the couch. 'You,' he said. 'What do you know about psychological shock? All you talk about is based on theory. How can you understand when you have no way of knowing?'

'You fool!' She slipped from the couch and stood facing him, burnished copper haloing the smooth contours of her face.

'Do you think you're the only one to have suffered? Listen! When I was a child of seven, I had something terrible happen to me. My family lived in an undersea farm. I was being transported from school back to home via a pressure tube. They're different now, but in those days they used to seal every individual in a transit capsule before shooting them along the tube. While in transit there was a minor earthquake. Nothing serious for those who lived on the surface, but hell itself for those in the farm. Stress fields cracked domes as if they had been eggshells. The tube was ruptured. The capsule I was in became tangled with wreckage. For fifteen hours I lay in that thing waiting to die.'

He watched as the sea-green eyes filled with tears.

'There was an air generator and it kept me alive, but I was a child of seven in an environment I couldn't really understand. The capsule was transparent. The tube had cracked so that I was caught facing towards the sea. Something was out there. A man had been caught in the implosion.

The pressure had squeezed his lungs out through his mouth and he hung there, caught, blowing a red balloon.'

She blinked, remembering. 'Fifteen hours,' she said. 'For a child, an eternity. When they rescued me, I was trying to escape. Not physically, that was impossible, but I did the only thing I could. Had they arrived later, I would have been an incurable catatonic.'

'You ran into the past,' he said. 'Found escape in what you thought was the safety of previous years. But no time is without stress.' Gently he reached out and touched her hair. It was silken in its smooth softness. 'But they found you,' he said. 'I'm glad of that.'

'Are you, Jules?' Her voice was as soft as her hair. He caught the odor of her perfume as she moved closer to him, the warmth of her body as he closed her in his arms. 'Do I mean something to you?'

'You mean a hell of a lot.' Deliberately, he stepped back and looked at her. 'As a woman, you — ' He broke off, frowning.

'Jules? What — '

'Quiet!' He stepped across the floor to

where the ventilator showed its grilled face. He lifted his hand before it, shook his head, wet his finger and tried again. 'There's no air circulating,' he said. 'Someone has cut the flow.'

'Is that serious?'

'Not while the gravity stays on. If they cut that too, we'll be in trouble.' He caught the question in her eyes. 'There are no convection currents in a gravity-free environment,' he explained. 'Unless the air is kept circulating you'll gather a cloud of vitiated air around your head. If you are asleep or unconscious, it will kill you by asphyxiation.' He held his moistened finger before the grill again. 'Nothing,' he said worriedly. Crossing to the speaker, he thumbed the button. 'Therapy to Control,' he said. 'Answer.'

Illraya joined him as he waited. 'Is that out, too?'

He thumbed the button again, not answering. 'Therapy to Control,' he snapped. 'Damn you! Respond! Is anyone on duty? Carmodine to Control!'

The silence grew, became something almost tangible, and then little sounds began to fill the atmosphere. Tiny noises inescapable from any functioning mechanism; the soft hum from the gravity plates in the deck, the transmitted vibration of distant movement, the sound of boots against metal, the pump of liquids in the hydroponic tanks. The ship held life and living things are rarely frozen in stasis. They move and, in a ship of space, noise can only be lost by dampened vibrations.

Head close to the bulkhead, Carmodine listened to the telltale sounds. He was intent, the hard planes of his face craggy with line and shadow, eyes narrowed as he tried to make sense from what he heard.

'Jules?'

He straightened, shaking his head. 'Nothing,' he admitted. 'But things aren't right. I wonder — ' He broke off, spinning to face the door of the cabin.

Metal clanged as it slammed open.

A crewman stood in the opening, blood on his face, a gun in his hand. He took one step forward, mouth working.

'Help . . . quick . . . they . . . ' He coughed and choked on a torrent of blood from punctured lungs, bright red, pulsing and then, as he fell, a turgid flood oozing thickly over the deck.

Outside, in the passage, a man screamed in dying anger.

4

Alone in space

Carmodine stooped, picked up the heavy pistol the crewman had dropped and kicked shut the cabin door. It had a lock. He threw the wards and stooped over the body, eyes and fingers gentle as he made a quick examination. Straightening, he shook his head.

'What's happening?' Illraya looked at the dead man, the locked door of the cabin. She flinched as a gun outside thundered a blast of energy. A gush of acrid heat filtered into the cabin. 'Jules!'

'I was wrong,' he said thickly. 'I gave them a week, but it was too much. The men have taken all they intend to. This is mutiny!'

Illraya looked at the man on the floor. 'Dead?'

'Yes.' He looked at the gun in his hand. It was flared with a swollen combustion chamber, cooling vanes running the length of the barrel. A flare-gun, designed to clear undergrowth, blast cleansing flame against contaminated surfaces. A short-range weapon which could incinerate a man. 'That's why they cut the air,' he said. 'Stopped it circulating. They broke into the Armoury and didn't want any transmitted sound to betray them.'

'Clever,' she commented. 'It took brains to think of that.'

'If spacemen were stupid, they wouldn't be spacemen,' said Carmodine curtly. He stood, thinking. 'Not all the crew can have mutinied. Brensco must have retained the loyalty of his officers and possibly his guards. They would be up in Control while the crew would be down in the engine room. That means we're caught in the middle.' He scowled, hefting the gun. 'Damn it,' he said. 'What a hell of a mess.'

'It isn't your fault, Jules,' she pointed out. 'You tried to warn Paul.'

'I should have tried harder.' He looked past her, examining the cabin. 'Listen,' he said. 'I'm going out. Lock the door after me and stay here until it's over.' He paused as sounds came from the speaker. 'They're trying to restore communication. Now remember, stay here until it's safe to leave.'

Outside, the corridor was silent, the smell of heat and blistered paint hanging in the air, smoke a dissipating cloud. Carmodine strained, listening. From the far end of the passage he caught a hint of sound and moved quickly towards it. Metal rang as a man eased himself into the corridor. He was armed. Carmodine stared into the pitted orifice of a gun.

'Who are you?'

'Carmodine. What's happened? Mutiny?'

The man nodded, sagging against the side of the passage. He was wounded, one arm hung uselessly at his side. 'Some of the men grabbed guns and tried to cut down the officers and guards. Brensco suspected it might happen, so we weren't caught totally unprepared, but we lost four dead and two badly wounded.' He paused, biting his lip from the pain of his blistered arm.

'Four dead,' said Carmodine quickly. 'Officers?'

'Guards.' The man made an effort to straighten. 'We can't spare them.' He slumped against the wall, face the colour of lead. 'Damn arm,' he whispered and then, 'Whose side are you on?'

'Yours.' Carmodine reached out and took the gun from the wounded man's hand. 'You need treatment. Where is Brensco now? In Control?'

The man nodded.

'And the men in the engine room?'

'Yes. I was trying to get away. Carson, too. They spotted us and let fly. I managed to hold them back, but not for long.' He groaned. 'My arm! For God's sake get me something to kill the pain.'

'Sure,' said Carmodine. His fist was a blur as he slammed it against the point of the man's jaw. He caught the unconscious man and gently eased him to the floor. It was rough, crude treatment, but the best he could do under the circumstances. 'You'll be all right,' he said to the unconscious man. 'At least you're alive.'

Not like his friend. Carson must have been the man who had died in Illraya's therapy room. Carmodine tucked both

63

guns into his waistband and stooped to pick up the man he had knocked out. First he would take him back to the cabin and then try his luck with the men.

He touched the body — and almost died in a gout of flame.

Instinct saved him. That of the click of metal, the hiss of indrawn breath, even the rasp of a boot on the metal of the deck. Frantically he sprang to one side, gagging on the stench of roasted flesh as he clawed at his waist.

On the humming deck plates the body of the wounded man glowed for a moment before slumping into ash. Carmodine lifted the barrel of his guns.

Thunder roared as he squeezed the triggers. Twin blasts of flaming energy seared down the corridor and turned the far bulkhead into a streaming wall of flame. A man shrieked and sprang into the open, frenziedly slapping at his burning clothes. He screamed once more and then died as Carmodine fired a second time.

The rolling echoes died and yielded to straining silence. Carmodine waited until only the hum of the deck plates reached his ears and then walked grimly down the passages leading to the engine room. Down there, men would be waiting, ready to play the most serious game in the universe — the game of life and death, with death the losers' share. His only hope was that they would regard him as a neutral.

He turned a corner and saw the head of a flight of stairs. He moved down them, saw a passage, a door, the sudden glint of metal. Fire and thunder roared, lashing over his head as he dropped, spraying the deck as he rolled. He twisted his left hand and sent flame back in answer. He rolled again, found a flimsy shelter behind the stairs and laid down a barrage of searing heat.

Inside the engine room, a frantic voice yelled above the rolling echoes. 'Hey, there! You, in the corridor!'

Carmodine eased his triggers.

'Who are you?'

Carmodine yelled back his name. 'Carmodine! You want to parley?'

'You're the prisoner, aren't you? The

one having treatment?' The voice paused as if conferring. 'Look, we don't like this. We're good Homogenetic League men, but that Brensco went too far. We want an inquiry. If Brensco will agree to make a deal, all right. But if he won't, we'll fight to the finish.'

Carmodine eased aching muscles. 'You're in a spot. Suppose Brensco won't agree to an inquiry?'

'He's got to. It's the law.'

'Federation law,' agreed Carmodine. 'But this is a League vessel and you're way out where there is no Federation. What I'm saying is, will you accept a compromise?' He was uncomfortable crouched behind the flimsy shelter of the stairs. Carefully he moved out, straightened, moved towards the engine room doors. Halfway there, he remembered and laid both guns on the deck plates in plain sight of anyone who might be watching. 'Well? How long are you going to take before making up your minds?'

'Take it easy,' said the voice. 'We've got to think about this.'

'You've got nothing to think about,'

snapped Carmodine. 'You can fight to the finish or make a deal. As far as I can see, you've got no choice.' He thought of something. 'Are you all in there?'

'That's our business.'

'That's right,' agreed Carmodine. He frowned, thinking of where else the mutineers could be. Logic dictated they be at the most vulnerable stations in the ship. He remembered the stoppage of circulating air. Power could be cut from many places and they didn't have to be in the air plant. Where, then? Close to the engine room because they would want each other's mutual support, but not too close, lest they both be taken at the same time. And somewhere protected.

The water tanks, of course. Where else?

'All right,' said the voice from within the engine room. 'We're willing to make a deal. Take word to Brensco and tell him that. Tell him to call a truce, forget the whole thing. There's dead on both sides, but we didn't start the shooting.' The voice hardened; 'If he wants to play it different, we'll fight until we drop and the last man blows the engines.'

'I'll tell him,' said Carmodine. 'Just don't do anything hasty.'

Brensco was in the control room. He glowered as Carmodine was ushered in by guards so jumpy that the big man could smell the stink of their terror. As expendable personnel, they would be the first to go if it came to an outright battle.

Brensco gestured their dismissal. 'You claim to have something to tell us. What is it?'

'I've brought you a message,' Carmodine said. 'From your crew, do you want to hear it?'

'From those mutinous dogs?' Brensco tightened his lips, cold eyes glittering with rage.

'From your crew,' said Carmodine patiently. 'They want you to call a truce. Do that and everything goes back to normal. Almost to normal,' he corrected himself. 'Nothing can replace the dead. Incidentally they claim that you started the shooting.'

'They lie!'

'Maybe. Anyway, I've delivered the message and now it's up to you.'

One of the officers on duty coughed.

'What would you advise?' he said.

'Advice is unnecessary and unwanted,' snapped Brensco before Carmodine could answer. 'They are crewmen while I am the captain. There can be no talk of compromise. They must yield. The ringleaders will be executed. There will be no truce.'

'Not unless you're sensible,' agreed Carmodine. 'I don't think those men are bluffing. And what can you do about it? You hold the Control Room, but what of it? What do you do when the lights go out, the gravity is cut? The heart of the ship lies with its power source, and you've lost that. You could lose more.' He told them of his suspicions. 'If I were the mutineers, that's exactly what I'd do. One party to hold the engine room and another to take care of the insurance. In this case, the water supply. If things get to the point of no return, they'll wreck the ship no matter what. Take the engine room and they'll contaminate the water. Safeguard the water and they'll destroy the motive power, if they don't blow up the vessel completely. Heads, they win; tails, we lose.'

'He's right,' said the officer who had spoken before. 'Captain, we've got to agree to some sort of a compromise. Once we get control of the ship, we can think again.'

'No,' said Carmodine emphatically. 'That's a crazy way to handle it. Try it and you're begging for trouble. If you make a deal, stick to it. If you don't want to play it that way, then you'll have to hit hard and be sure of winning the first time.'

'But how?' The officer looked baffled. 'If we go against them, those in the water compartments will have time to ruin our supply.'

'Can't you hit them both at once?' Carmodine glared his impatience. 'Where are the plans of this vessel? Let's see what can be done.'

Brensco hesitated, then nodded his permission. Carmodine had once held his own command. As an officer, ex-officer, he could have no real sympathy with mutiny. And, Brensco realized, he needed all the help he could get.

'It's possible,' said Carmodine an hour later. His finger traced a path on the sheaf of plans. 'There is an external port leading to the pumps. A party could go through it and down into the central inspection tube. That's where they'll be, if anywhere. At the same time, a party can make a diversionary attack on the engine room. When everything is ready, go in and hit them front and rear. If you have some anaesthetic gas, it would make the job even more simple.'

'We have the gas,' said Brensco. 'Emergency supplies.' He narrowed his eyes at the mesh of lines and symbols. 'But there's no entrance where you say. That's the reloading hatch. It's blocked by the pumps. We'd have to cut our way through a mass of machinery before we could get through.'

An officer wearing the insignia of an engineer reluctantly agreed. 'The Captain's right, Carmodine. That way is out.' His finger tapped the plans. 'It might be possible to cut a plate out of the hull and get in that way. We'd have to seal it after, but that wouldn't be too hard.'

'Where would that lead?'

'Close to the pump. There's a waste

71

space between the wall of the tank and the inner hull. Not much, but enough to let a man crawl through.' He pursed his lips as he brooded over the plans. 'Now, if an opening were cut just here, it might be possible to drill a hole into the space beyond. Fit it with a gas distributor and, with luck, they'll be flat before they know it.' He looked at the faces ringing the desk. 'It'll mean going outside, of course.'

'I'll lead the party,' said Brensco.

'No, you won't,' said Carmodine. 'The men in the engine room will expect you to contact them. If you're not around, they'll get suspicious. The only one who can be spared is someone they don't know and won't expect to hear from.' He met their eyes. 'Yes,' he said flatly. 'Me. I'm not crew and I'm not an officer. I'm a prisoner on this vessel and I don't want to cooperate. So I'm going to bed and I'm going to stay there until this thing is all settled.'

Bed, he thought an hour later, was a peculiar place. A harshly lit annex room with spacesuits racked on the walls like medieval suits of armour and, like the old armour, they served the same purpose, which was to protect the life of the man within.

Mason, the officer-engineer, took painstaking care as he fitted Carmodine into a suit.

'You should let me come with you,' he said. 'It's going to take more than one man to do what you intend.'

'You've only got one man,' said Carmodine bluntly. 'The rest of you are known. We've got no choice in the matter. But thanks all the same.' Carmodine checked the helmet instruments. Air and battery power were at optimum. At his feet rested a bundle wrapped in iron-sprayed synthetic and containing the cylinders of anaesthetic gas together with a heavy-duty laser cutting torch. The torch was portable and its power should be enough to do the job. Carmodine had a spare just in case.

'Make certain your line is snug,' fussed Mason. He jerked at the nylon rope. 'Double-check after fastening and before moving off. Don't lift both feet off the hull at the same time. Slide your boots.

Don't try to walk normal. Keep your . . . '

'All right,' said Carmodine, suddenly impatient. 'I know you mean well, but I have been outside in a suit before. And we haven't all the time in the world,' he added quickly in order to soften his rebuff. 'Brensco can't stall them forever.' He jerked his chin to operate the suit radio. The 'ON' light flashed and he switched it off. 'I'll signal as soon as I'm ready.'

'You'll stay in radio contact all the time,' said Mason sharply. 'That's an order. The mutineers won't be able to hear you, but we can. And we have to,' he reminded. 'The whole plan depends on timing.'

He watched as Carmodine sealed his helmet and walked to the inner door of the airlock. It closed behind him. Pumps whined as they withdrew the air. As they fell silent, a red lamp flashed from a signal light above.

Carmodine was alone in space.

5

The attack

There was beauty in the great emptiness, but it was a harsh, remote thing of tremendous spaces and scattered lights, of drifting curtains and sheets of luminescence, clouds of nighted dust and reaching spirals dusted with the glowing gems of stars.

It took a man and made him small, a speck of dirt in the immensity of the universe, an insignificant mote of quivering jelly, helpless against the titanic forces all around. And yet these same forces made him demand to be greater than he was; to be recognized as a creature whose mind could create the things that threatened to engulf his identity.

Carmodine stood in the open port looking at the universe through the open door. Within the helmet, he could hear the soft hiss of air coming from the tanks.

He could hear, if he listened, the beat of his heart and the roar of blood in his ears. And he could hear the rasp of his own breathing.

Sounds that comprised his personal world.

He drew a deep breath, consciously fighting against the attraction of stars like diamonds, a scatter of gems, distances that became meaningless with endless zeros. He moved and heard the faint scrape of his boot against the metal of the hull. The boots were magnets clinging to the ferrous alloy. The elbows of his suit were other magnets, and there were more at his knees. The metal-sprayed fabric of the bundle clung to his belt, weightless now, away from the gravity-plates in the decks.

Carmodine gripped the edges of the open portal, threw his body forward, altered balance as he slid first one boot, then the other over the outer edge and onto the skin of the actual hull. For a brief moment, the stars whirled before his eyes and then he was standing upright on the hull, the open port a gaping hole at his rear.

He lifted his head and felt, as he always did at such times, the stomach-wrenching acrophobia which brought sudden and terrible panic.

He was going to fall!

There was nothing to stop him. To either side, the hull curved sharply away. Another curve ran from nose to gaping venturis. He was balanced precariously on a surface that seemed as smooth as glass and to each side, waiting, sprawled the bottomless pit of the universe. He was going to fall! There was nothing to stop him! He couldn't help but fall!

Some men never felt it, but they were few. A substantial proportion couldn't rid themselves of it and were useless to man the ships traversing the void. The rest felt, but were able to master, the instinctive fear by using cold logic, experience and icy nerve to accept what every instinct screamed was wrong.

They wouldn't fall. They couldn't. Without power, a ship coasted. There was no spin to hurl them away by centrifugal force. Unless they deliberately kicked themselves free, they would remain attached to the hull by magnetic attraction. Even if they did drift away from the curved surface, they would only ride alongside. The only real danger was that they might kick too hard, throw themselves away from the ship so fast that the minute gravitational attraction of the vessel would be too weak to hold them.

Then, unless they could get back, they would be lost for eternity.

Carmodine had no intention of facing that danger. He knelt, slowly, letting the magnets in the knees of his suit clamp against the hull. From a reel on his belt, he pulled a line and fastened the end to the bundle. On hands and knees, sliding one pair of limbs after the other, he worked his way down and around the hull.

He was being cautious, but with reason. Already he had taken one risk by not attaching his line, shedding the precaution for the sake of easier manoeuverability, but speed was essential. That and a close scrutiny of the hull. The ship was strange, and plans that looked one thing in the glolight of a cabin seemed to bear no relation to the ship itself when crawling on the hull beneath the light of stars.

He paused, orientating himself. He had worked his way in a fifty-degree angle a good hundred degrees around the ship. This line of progress should take him to where a series of eyebolts ringed the hull for just such an eventuality as outside repairs while in transit. If he could find them, head directly aft until he found the third letter of their markings, then move twenty feet to the right, he should be over the exact spot where he had to cut.

He tensed, splaying arms and legs, pressing his suit against the hull as sweat started to trickle from his forehead and ran stinging into his eyes.

Had the ship moved?

It had felt like it. For one dreadful second he had thought the vessel had dropped, moved away from him, rather. A trifling notion, probably born of fear. No matter how logical a man could be, the age-old fear of falling still remained. He blinked the sweat from his eyes and sucked air deep into his chest. At times like this, a man needed the company of trusted friends.

He rose a little and unclipped the line from the bundle. He drew it out and snapped the end over one of the eyebolts, angry at himself for neglecting the precaution. Limbs extended, he crawled over the hull looking for memorized identification. This plate? That one?

He closed his eyes, willing himself mentally back to the control room, seeing again the plans spread before him. Mason's remembered voice was a thin echo. 'Find this spot first. Move twenty feet to the right as you're facing the tubes. There's an eyebolt. Five feet from that is a hatch. Strike a diagonal to your right and twenty feet down is the place to cut. Cross-check by taking a sight on the markings. Third down and twenty feet to the right.'

He reared upright and stared around. There was the third letter of the markings. Two steps forward and one to the right and he should be positioned just right. He squatted down and opened the bundle. The gas cylinders he put to one side, together with the spare laser. The other he picked up and triggered into life. A spot glowed on the burnished metal, widened, turned from cherry red to eye-searing blue-white, grew into a line as Carmodine moved the laser. A cloud of brilliant flecks rose from the cut, vaporized metal blasted free by its own released gas.

Carmodine dropped another filter and leaned closer. The vaporized metal settled on the darkened plastic and made it even more opaque. He swore and wiped at the plastic. A careless move of the torch and he would send the beam slicing into his own suit. He changed the direction of the beam and sent it in a ragged circle. The disc of metal lifted a little as he finally cut it free. He caught it, moved it to one side and set it down beside the gas cylinders. On his gloved palm, tiny flecks of molten alloy sparkled for a moment. In space, it took time for heat to dissipate.

A voice whispered from the radio in his helmet. 'Carmodine, this is Mason. How are you doing?'

'I'm through the outer hull. Is Brensco

managing to stall them along?'

'So far, he's managed. You were right about them wanting to check on the officers. We've all had to talk to them in turn. Anything you want me to do?'

'One thing,' said Carmodine. 'Take care of the woman. Illraya is in the therapy room. Try and get her up with you in control.'

'I'll do it,' said Mason. 'Yell if you need anything.'

The radio fell silent.

Carmodine stripped off the ruined filter and stooped to look into the hole he had cut out of the hull. The edges were rough, irregular, but they were dangerously sharp and might gash his suit. He straightened, and reached for the gas cylinders and spare laser. He checked the torch and thrust it into the hole. The cylinders followed and, after them, Carmodine. He thrust himself forward, the helmet light throwing a clear disc of radiance. It showed the space between the hulls, the airtight cross-members that divided the space between the hulls into individual compartments. He had cut through the outer skin very close to where two of the thick stanchions joined. A few inches to one side and he would have had the entire job to do again.

Crouched in the limited space, he looked at the inner skin. Beyond it would be the water tank, the one that had a space between its wall and the inner hull. If he cut another hole, squeezed through and made his way along the wall of the tank towards the inner tube, all he would then have to do would be to release the gas in the cylinders. But if he penetrated the inner skin, the air within the ship would immediately begin to escape. A blast of molten droplets from the cut would splatter against his suit. Warnings would sound and emergency doors would seal off this particular section. The mutineers would be alerted and the whole plan aborted.

Carmodine nudged the 'SEND' switch of his radio.

'Mason?'

'Here,' answered the engineer immediately. 'Trouble?'

'A question. I'm between the hulls in

sector . . . ' Carmodine shone his light on painted numerals on the cross-members, ' . . . B56. Am I in the right spot?'

A moment of silence, and then, 'Right smack on the nose. Are you ready to drill for the gas?'

'I've been thinking. If I remember the plan, there is an emergency door a little forward of here, right?'

'I'll check,' said Mason. 'Give me a couple of minutes.'

He was back in just over one. 'You're right. There's a chance you might burn a hole right smack into the jamb. However, if you go aft and to the right of the compartment you're in, you'll be well clear.'

'Yes,' said Carmodine, thinking. 'Listen,' he said. 'I'm going to try something. If I can seal the hull behind me, I can feed gas into both sides of the door. That way, we'll stand a chance of knocking out all the mutineers in both sections. Are the blowers working yet?'

'Yes. That was the first thing Brensco demanded . . . full resumption of normal air circulation as a proof of good faith. It didn't cost them anything to agree. They need fresh air as much as we do.'

Mason was cynical, Carmodine equally so. 'Make sure you seal their area off from the main distribution. We're not greedy . . . they can have every molecule of gas to themselves. Tell Brensco to get ready to attack. I'm going to start drilling almost right away.' He hesitated. 'The woman, Illraya. Did you manage to get her up to control?'

'Not yet,' said Mason. 'But I've spoken with her over the intercom. She's safe enough where she is.'

'All right,' said Carmodine. 'I'll let you know when I'm feeding in the gas.'

Cautiously he turned and thrust his helmet up through the hole in the outer skin. Magnets held elbows and knees to the hull as he reached for the discarded sheet of metal-sprayed fibre and the removed plate of the hull. He dragged them towards him. The section had been cut more oval than circular, so it was easy to pass the segment through the hole. The fabric followed. Carmodine paused as he remembered his safety line. Unclipping it from his belt, he threw the reel clear. Ducking, he gripped the fabric, spread it and laid it over the hole. Twisting the plate, he managed to wedge it back into the opening, the fabric blocking the cut made by the laser.

Picking up the torch, he adjusted the beam and played it on the wedged material. He had enough spare fabric to supply material for a thin weld all around the cut. It wasn't strong, but it wasn't intended to be. If it would remain airtight for a short while, he would be satisfied.

Each gas cylinder had a specially adapted nozzle so that a hole could be drilled and the nozzle fitted with the minimum loss of air. In theory, that was. Almost too late Carmodine had remembered the unsuspected forces waiting below. The atmosphere of the ship was at fifteen pounds per square inch. Once a hole had been drilled, it would blast out in a vicious stream. Without the hampering confines of the suit, he would probably have been able to fit the nozzle against such pressures. Wearing the suit, he wasn't so sure.

The laser threw a searing beam against the inner hull in the far corridor. It glowed with the sparkling of released gases, the molten droplets of vaporized metal. The sparkling fountain became a stream, a sudden, furious gush. Carmodine threw aside the torch and grabbed at the nozzle of one of the cylinders. He jabbed it into the hole, using the strength of both arms. Air whined around him as it rushed from the compartment below, filling the narrow space between the hulls. The outer seal held.

The emergency doors were set to operate at a drop of three pounds per square inch of internal pressure. Carmodine was gambling that the air loss would compensate without the trips being activated; that the combined air pressure of the compartment into which he had drilled and the space in which he crouched would equalize above the twelve pound level.

He was sweating as he rammed the nozzle home and spun the wheel to lock the device into place. Immediately, without turning on the gas, he snatched up the laser and crawled to the far compartment to drill a second hole. Fitting the nozzle was much easier this time.

Carmodine hit the switch of his radio. 'Mason?'

'Here.' The engineer was sitting on top of the radio. 'Is everything all right?'

'Couldn't be better.' Carmodine wished that he could wipe his face. Exertion had coupled with normal body heat to raise his temperature and he felt as if he were in an oven. 'Both gas tanks fitted,' he said. 'I'm ready to feed it to them. Is Brensco ready to do his part?'

'Perfectly ready, Jules.' The captain's cold tones replaced the warm humanity of the engineer. 'We are ready to attack and will hit five seconds after you have fed in the gas.'

'Have you sealed the area?'

'Certainly.'

Carmodine hesitated. 'The mutineers,' he said. 'Are they suspicious?'

'I don't think so. I have been talking to them, keeping them occupied.' Brensco's voice became savage. 'Bargaining with them as if they were equals. Haggling as if we were fishwives on a wharf.'

'It's gained time,' said Carmodine. 'Who's talking to them now?'

'The woman,' said Brensco. 'Doctor Samorova.'

'Illraya?' Carmodine felt uneasy. 'Why? What made them want to talk to her?'

'It was my suggestion,' said Brensco. 'Why not? She's a psychiatrist, and a good one. Also she is a woman and men are always more interested in the sound of a female voice than that of a male. She is soothing them, Jules. Feeding them pap. Getting them ready for the execution.' Brensco laughed. 'I am, of course, speaking metaphorically, Jules. I do not really intend to execute them. At least not all of them.'

'I don't think it would be wise to kill any of them,' said Carmodine curtly. 'They are your crew. You need them. Pluto isn't the place to go if you have no friends.'

'Friends?' Brensco's voice was brittle with mockery. 'Where are they now, Jules? What good did they do you? More importantly, what good did you do them?

To quote an old saying, 'With you for a friend, who needs an enemy'?' He chuckled. 'Don't worry about the mutineers, Jules. They aren't worried about you. They've only asked to speak to you twice.'

'When was that?' Carmodine felt the muscles knot along the edge of his jaw. 'Damn you, Paul! Answer me! How long ago?'

'Not long.' Brensco sounded surprised at the violence of Carmodine's reaction. 'They asked to speak to you and they were told that you were asleep. A short while ago they asked again and were given the same answer. I can't see why . . . '

'You blind fool!' Carmodine reached for the control on the gas cylinder. 'They asked after me and you gave them an answer like that? Told them I was asleep when Illraya's talking to them from the very room in which I'm supposed to be?'

Mason caught the significance. 'They'll ask her. All she has to do is call you.' He hesitated. 'More than that. They can boost the gain and hear everything in the room. Your breathing. The echo of your heartbeat, even.' He swallowed. 'Maybe they haven't thought of it yet,' he said encouragingly. 'We still have time.'

Time!

How long before the mutineers guessed that someone was outside the vessel?

Guessed the reason and did something about it?

From the engine room they could ignite the tubes!

'Start the attack,' he ordered. 'I'm feeding the gas now!'

Brensco was sharp. 'Wait! We're not wholly ready. There's a . . . '

'Do it!' interrupted Carmodine savagely. His hand twisted the valve on the cylinder. 'There's no time to waste. Jump them now! Hurry!'

The valve opened. He crawled to the other cylinder and sent its contents gushing through the nozzle into the air of the compartment beneath. It would spread between the wall of the water tank and down into the central tube. It would spread through the ventilators as the blowers carried it to the engine room. With luck it would be all that was needed.

But he knew they wouldn't have that kind of luck. The mutineers were too shrewd. They would have taken the obvious precaution of closing the emergency doors between the party at the tanks and those at the engines. Locked and closed them tight against unforeseen eventualities.

Carmodine knew he was being pessimistic. The chance of the crew having thought of every possibility was remote. Spacemen did not go outside for the fun of it. Without the plans, they couldn't guess at the danger from such a quarter. They would be talking, arguing, pressing their claims. They would be listening to the softly feminine and smoothly professional voice of the psychiatrist. Illraya would keep them listening, freeze them with semantic magic as Brensco moved in to the attack.

Carmodine relaxed. There was nothing for him to worry about. All he had to do was to stay put until it was all over and then retrace his steps back to the open port.

But if Brensco failed . . . ?

Missed his chance . . . ?

Carmodine glanced at the gauges within his helmet. His air was lower than he'd thought. The work had taken longer than he'd guessed. But he still had enough and, if the worst came, he could always burn his way through the inner hull. He moved forward to where he'd thrown the laser. His back lifted as he crawled over the plates.

The ship pulsed!

It was as if something gigantic had kicked the ship in the rear. Carmodine jerked towards the lower part of the section and, as he passed beneath the patched hull, the crude seal blasted free.

Air blasted through the opening. Caught in the vicious gust, Carmodine felt himself jerked from the metal on which he skidded. The edge of the hole smashed against the air tank on his back. Something caught, then yielded with a rasp of metal.

Like a pea spat from a tube, Carmodine was flung from the ship into the void.

He spun, cartwheeling, catching flashing glimpses of stars, the ship, more stars.

Light blazed from the massed splendour of the Milky Way. More light glared from the instrument panel below the faceplate.

Something hit his helmet, rasped as it slid aside. He grasped at it, clamping his hands on something thin and flexible, feeling a sudden jar as they met something hard and unyielding. Hands locked, he felt the tremendous jerk at his wrists, his arms, tearing at his shoulders and sending more stars dancing in his eyes. But those came from his brain and, unless he could hold on, they could be the last he ever saw.

Abruptly the cartwheeling stopped and was replaced by a longitudinal spinning as if he were a top balanced on his feet. He threw back his hand and looked along the line of his arms. His gloved hands were hard against a small drum, from which extended a short length of line. The rest of the rope extended from the drum to the ship. It was straight and still seemed to be quivering.

Carmodine gusted his breath in a great lung-emptying sigh of relief. He had been dead, though still able to see and hear and breathe. Then a miracle! The line he'd thrown from him when he'd plugged the hole in the hull had unwound itself from the reel and had hung in space, waiting.

His bruised hands tightened convulsively on the rope. It was his life. If it broke, if he lost contact with it, then he would be dead again and there would be no second miracle.

Slowly, carefully, he heaved on the thin line. It was made of synthetics and had a breaking strain which was incredible for its thickness, but against the stars it seemed as fragile as gossamer. Sweat ran over his face, filling his eyes with salty burning, and his lungs ached from tension. Still revolving so that the universe raced before his eyes, he pulled himself up to the reel. He tasted blood as he forced himself to release one hand. It was numb, hard to manage, and he guessed at pulped flesh and shattered bones. He pulled again, using the reel as a fulcrum and managed to grip the rope between his legs. Praying, he let go of the line.

Nothing happened. He didn't fall or lose the rope. He gulped and fought for air. Slowly he caught hold of the short end of the line beyond the reel and tried to hook it to his belt. His fingers were rebels in love with suicide. He snarled, suddenly mad with rage at their refusal to obey. He tried again, concentrating until the veins throbbed on his temples and blood roared in his ears.

The hook entered the ring. Hesitated and finally snapped home.

For the first time, Carmodine had time to think.

The ship had pulsed. It could only have been due to the engines firing, blasting energy from the venturis, to jerk the ship into sudden acceleration. Either the mutineers had done it or it had been a result of the radar scanning devices picking up a scrap of space debris and kicking the vessel out of its way.

If the reason had been the latter, Carmodine could now relax. Debris was rare in space at the best of times. Out here, the odds against meeting anything dangerous from such a source were astronomical. For the danger to be real was possible only in the wildest speculations of random probabilities.

But if the mutineers had deliberately fired the engines, they had done it either as a threat to Brensco or because they hoped to do exactly what they had done. They had thrown Carmodine off the ship as a man would flick an annoying insect from his sleeve.

Now it was up to him to get back.

Automatically he scanned the instruments of his suit. The tiny panel was glowing with warning lights. The suit had been weakened in three places. The internal temperature was too high. The air tanks were exhausted.

Exhausted?

He remembered the blow as he had hit the edge of the hole, the harsh grating noise, both temporarily forgotten. The tanks were empty. The only air he had was that within his suit.

He chinned the radio switch. 'Mason,' He called. 'Mason! Anyone! Can you hear me?'

He heard nothing but the sound of his

own heart, his own breathing.

'Mason. Carmodine here. I need help, and fast. Bring me some air. Mason! Anyone? I need help!'

He was still spinning and faced the wrong way down the rope. His feet were pointed towards the ship and that wouldn't do. It was easier to pull than push. He bent, grabbed the line, pulled as he kicked his legs out behind him. Now he could see the vessel, clear against the background of stars, little shimmers coming from the burnished hull. He reached out, caught the rope and pulled himself along it. Without weight and only mass to take care of, it wasn't too hard. Had he plenty of air, it would have been easy, a routine manoeuver in space training. But he had no air, the rope was a long one and he was fighting the screaming agony of his smashed hands.

The ship pulsed again.

He saw it. Saw the mouths of the venturis suddenly glow and spit dancing tongues of flame, a savage blossom of heat and light and naked energy. The ship jerked forward as if it were a can kicked by a boy. Carmodine on the end of his line was jerked after it.

He couldn't hold on. The rope made a thin whine as it ripped through his helpless fingers, the sound eerie in the confines of his suit. The reel hit his legs, grated over his stomach and slammed against his battered hands. Slammed against them and past them as it hurried after the ship.

He screamed as his belt tore at his waist, almost ripping him apart, and then, as it held and his own inertia yielded, the fastened rope dragged him after it like a hooked fish.

Contrary actions met and were balanced by the immutable laws of physics. Carmodine, at the end of the rope, was jerked like a weight at the end of a leash. He swung down and outward, still spinning, sweeping in a huge arc directly across the mouths of the giant venturis.

He caught glimpses of them, knowing that if they fired again he would be incinerated and spread across the galaxy as motes of impalpable dust. He felt the change of direction as the rope hit the snip, again as he was shot forward toward the bulk of the vessel.

He had one last glimpse of the hull rising to meet him and then there was a shooting impact, stars, pain and, abruptly, nothing at all.

6

Memories

There was a bleak plain of ice and driving snow and a thin, viciously cold wind. In the distance shone a red spark as if of fire and Carmodine made towards it. Abruptly he was there, standing on a hummock looking down at the fire. Men clustered around the blaze but they kept their faces hidden and looked shapeless beneath heavy garments. Carmodine stared at them and wondered who they were and why he was here.

The sky split with rolling thunder that echoed across the plain, reverberated and became a voice commanding him to stare at the sunless sky. The darkness seemed to press down on him so that he shivered and moved towards the fire. He knelt beside it, warming his hands, almost touching one of the huddled figures.

The man turned and looked at him.

Evans!

Carmodine reached out to touch the man but his hands wouldn't obey. He looked at them. They were both enclosed in a lump of ice. He held the ice close to the fire and felt heat and pain.

The ice dissolved, fell from his hands and he jerked to his feet. Again the thunder rolled across the sky, became a voice roaring at him to look up . . . up . . . up to the featureless sky.

Instead, he looked at the other men huddled around the fire. They moved, turning slowly so as to face him and sat watching as he looked. He knew them all. The faces belonged to old friends and he smiled and made as if to touch them. Pain stabbed both hands and, with the pain, the faces of the men he knew changed, became skulls glowing red with the reflection of the flames. The skulls grinned and they reached for him with hands like claws. In the bony sockets, eyes glowed red with hate.

The claws gripped him, sinking into his flesh, tearing, hot with pain.

Carmodine yelled and pushed at them,

struggling to escape their iron grip, smashing his hands against the redly gleaming bone. He jerked free, stepped back and was suddenly falling into a bottomless pit of ebon darkness.

A man stood at the edge of the pit and stared down, his face a miniature moon against the star-flecked sky.

Evans!

Carmodine choked as something engulfed him, lifted him, spewed him from the pit and out to the bleak plain. He ran, feet slipping on the ice, falling, picking himself up to run again, never seeming to make progress.

A man stood before him, tall and dark against the ghost light of the plain.

Evans!

Carmodine shrieked with pain and terror, screamed and beat his temples with his clenched fists. The thin wind keened over the plain, a strange wind, one that incorporated human voices and, like an animal, he spun and glared his defiance.

Something gripped his arms, his wrists, piled weight down on his chest and clogged his breathing. He struggled, struck out, felt the wind rise around him and, as if from a great distance, heard the screams of dying men.

'Carmodine!'

He groaned and fought the phantoms of his dreams.

'Carmodine! Wake up, man! Wake up!'

Acrid smoke stung his nostrils, rose within his skull to burst in a soundless explosion, shattering the world of imagery in which he wandered. Painfully he opened his eyes. The seamed face of Mason filled his visual world.

'Doctor Samorova! He's awake!'

Carmodine blinked at the engineer.

'I was just about giving up hope,' said Mason. 'The doctor said you'd be all right, but I wanted to be sure. How do you feel?'

Carmodine swallowed, forced words from his throat. 'I'll let you know when I find out,' he promised. 'Illraya?'

'Here, Jules.' Her face joined that of the engineer. Her eyes were bright and shining. Her lower lip was swollen as if from the bruising impact of teeth. Carmodine recalled a habit she had revealed during their sessions; when worried or anxious, she bit her lower lip. 'Thirsty?'

He nodded.

'Have some of this. When you've drunk it, you can sit up and start acting human again.' She laughed at his expression. 'I've had you in deep-sleep therapy for weeks now. Your bones are healed and so are your bruises. Mason has been coming in to give you massage and isometric exercises. He used a galvanic shock technique perfected by the Institute. You should be in perfect physical condition.' Her eyes narrowed as they searched his face. 'Look at me,' she demanded. 'At my left ear . . . the right . . . the top of my head . . . my chin. Now stare into my right eye . . . my left . . . the right again.' She made satisfied noises. 'Lift your right arm and touch your right ear . . . now the left. Lift them both together and touch your fingertips over the top of your head. Good. Once more. That's right.'

She looked at Mason. 'Patient ready for discharge.'

'Thank you, Doctor,' he said solemnly.

'You've done a fine job.'

Carmodine had to agree. Aside from a slight momentary nausea when he first stood upright, he seemed as good as new. Curiously he looked at his hands.

'They were pretty badly smashed,' said Mason, noticing his interest. 'And that wasn't all.'

'I was outside,' said Carmodine, remembering. 'I hit the hull.' He narrowed his eyes. 'The ship pulsed,' he said. 'The tubes were fired at least twice. What happened?'

'The mutineers guessed that something was wrong. I don't know just why. Maybe they sensed they were being stalled or they couldn't stomach not being able to talk to you. They could even have picked up silence where they'd expected to hear sound. If you had been with Doctor Samorova they would have known it.' Mason pursed his lips and shrugged. 'Who knows? I think that perhaps they were hoping to dig a spur into Brensco, remind him that they still held the ace. So they triggered the rocket tubes and gave the ship a kick in the rear.'

'I know,' said Carmodine grimly. 'I was in a position to have a good view.'

'Brensco was attacking by then,' continued the engineer. 'He went in and nothing could stop him. The second pulse came just as he reached the inner section of the engine room.' Mason glanced at the woman where she stood. 'Then we just went outside and brought you in.'

'He went outside,' she interrupted, pointing at Mason. 'He was suited up and ready to go. He heard you call for air and was adjusting an extra tank when the second pulse came.' Illraya smiled at the engineer. 'He went down and landed badly. Later I found a couple of cracked ribs. He's all right now.'

Carmodine looked at the woman. 'And?'

'Nothing,' said Mason. 'Forget it.'

'He went outside and brought you in,' said Illraya steadily. 'He was hurt, uncertain if the rockets would fire again or not, but he went outside just the same. If he hadn't, you would be dead by now. You had internal injuries, bad haemorrhages, a serious concussion. And you had no air. Five minutes,' she added. 'It was that close.'

'Too close,' said Carmodine with feeling. He remembered how he had felt while spinning helplessly in the void. 'I owe you my life,' he said to the engineer. 'I won't forget that.'

'You would have done the same,' said the engineer. He looked uncomfortable. 'In a way, you saved the lives of us all. Those mutineers meant business. They had rigged the engines for destruction. Brensco got to them just in time.'

Carmodine drew a deep breath. 'We're alive,' he said. 'That's the main thing.' He stretched, feeling and enjoying the interplay of sinew and muscles. He turned at the sound of pouring liquid.

Illraya gestured with the bottle. 'A celebration,' she said. 'Wine from the Grosso. I think the occasion calls for it.' She handed a glass to Mason, another to Carmodine, lifted a third for herself. 'Who can think of a toast?'

'To luck,' said Mason immediately. 'Without it, what are we? Where would we be?'

'I'll second that,' said Carmodine.

They drank and she refilled the glasses.

'Now you, Jules. It's your turn to give a toast.'

Carmodine frowned, thinking. 'To success,' he said. 'In everything we do.'

Again Illraya poured wine.

'To love,' she said as they lifted their glasses. 'To love,' she repeated.

Carmodine met her eyes, read their message. 'To love,' he agreed.

They drank.

Mason left, sensing the atmosphere, suddenly remembering duties he had neglected for too long.

Illraya poured more wine and sat beside Carmodine in the therapy couch. He sipped, tasting spiced chillness, sipped again as the wine lit fires in his soul. He felt alive again, warm with human passion and desire.

Illraya leaned forward and took the glass from his hand. She set it down beside her own.

'Jules,' she said. 'I love you. You must know that.'

He could admire her directness if not her wisdom.

'At first I thought it might be a simple

biological reaction,' she said calmly. 'The mating instinct, if you want to call it that. A physical need easily satisfied. But I was wrong. Nursing you all this time, I learned that. The way I felt when you were outside. When the ship pulsed and I thought that you were dead, I realized that it was a deeper thing than the need for physical release. Nursing you only confirmed that realization. I love you, Jules. I shall always love you.'

She moved. He felt the strength of her arms, smelled the scent of her hair, its silken touch against his cheek. Her lips touched his; honeyed butterflies perfumed with spiced wine. 'My darling,' she breathed softly. 'Jules, my darling.'

They kissed.

And, after a long while, she poured them both more wine.

'We've drunk to luck, success and love,' she said, eyes sparkling. 'What remains?'

'Hope,' he said.

'The future,' she corrected. 'We'll drink to them both.'

They drank and he looked at his glass. 'Illraya . . . '

'Don't say it, Jules,' she interrupted. 'I know the situation, but what of it? Pluto lies ahead. A lot can happen before we return home. We can clear your memory. With luck, we can even wipe clear the past.'

Carmodine shook his head. 'Brensco would never allow it. He will never forget that I deserted my command and he will never let others forget it, either. We are enemies. Why should he do me a favour? Does the lion lie down with the lamb?'

'Don't quote at me,' she said with mock severity. 'If you do, I can quote right back at you. 'The evil of a day is sufficient to that day'. It's a sensible way of looking at things. We are here now, together. Let us enjoy what we have. Who can be certain if we have a future?'

'No one,' he agreed, and then, to change the subject, 'What happened about the mutiny? I gather Brensco won, but what then?'

'He shot four men,' she said quietly. 'He claimed they were the ringleaders and gunned them down. He would have shot more, but his own officers stopped him.'

'And then?'

'He is operating the ship on a skeleton crew. The rest of the men are locked in one of the storage compartments and he says he is going to keep them imprisoned until we arrive at our destination.'

'Anything else?'

'I'm not sure,' she said slowly. 'I have a suspicion that he's taking drugs. I've seen him when he acts like a stranger. He is under tremendous psychological stress, Jules. He has been since the start of this journey. He cannot admit the slightest possibility of failure. Paranoia, schizophrenia, periods of hysteria followed by bouts touching the edge of manic depression . . . I've noted signs of them all. A classic case of adaptive breakdown.'

Carmodine looked puzzled. 'Are you saying that Brensco is insane?'

'In a clinical sense, yes,' she insisted. 'You must realize that I am talking about aberrations which are not a part of his normal psychological climate. In short, I'm saying that the captain has failed to maintain his adaptation to this environment. First the paranoia,' she ticked one finger. 'Delusions of grandeur coupled with the inevitable conviction that he was in danger. His life was in danger because others envied his godlike power. So he removed himself from as much human contact as possible and, by so doing, bolstered his delusion. The mutiny, naturally, proved that he was right to be fearful. Now he is afraid to do anything for fear it should be the wrong thing. Drugs, which could help, are abused because he is taking too large a dose or the wrong kind of drug.'

'Can't you help him?'

'Certainly I can. He needs rest and therapy and an undistorted view of the reality of things. But how can I treat him when he will let no one approach?' She ticked the last finger and snapped shut her hand. 'All we can do is wait. He will either get worse, try to escape into catatonia, or begin to mend. If we reach Pluto soon enough, he will begin to mend. The transition will probably be remarkable.'

Carmodine drank the last of his wine. 'He will effect a complete cure? Be just as he was?'

The woman shook her head. 'That is

doubtful. He will no longer be morose, that is safe to claim, but I don't think he will be as he was of old. More, I hesitate to say. All we can be certain about is that the probability of his values having changed is very high.'

'A distortion of the personality?' Carmodine thought about it, trying to imagine Brensco other than what he knew. It seemed impossible for the coldly dedicated man of science to be other than that. Warmth and human failings were alien to his character. 'I can't imagine it,' he admitted. 'But I suppose the possibility is always there.'

'Always,' she said, and then, casually, 'Tell me about Evans.'

'He was my old engineer,' said Carmodine immediately. 'I told you about him. He saved my life when we were caught in a storm on Jupiter. A good man. One of the best ever to have lived.' His voiced slowed, thickened. 'I loved that man like a father. He came with me to Pluto. He trusted me to take him to the edge of the Big Dark and get him safely back home.

'I killed him.'

Glass splintered in his hands. Silently, Illraya reached out and took the jagged pieces. With a wad of tissue, she wiped away the fragments and then threw both glass and tissue into the disposal chute. 'You killed him,' she said quietly. 'How did you do that?'

'Forget it.'

'I need to know,' she insisted. 'Tell me.'

'We'd landed,' he said rapidly, as if trying to spit out the words before some shutter clamped down in his mind. 'We'd settled the ship and had adopted exploratory routine. You know the sort of thing; the collecting of samples, the search for minerals and the taking of sample cores from deep drillings. It was hard work, but we liked it. We were happy enough and, always, there was the prospect of finding something really new. Artifacts, even. We used to make guesses about it. We even had a pot going for the one who found the first signs of previous habitation. Kid stuff, really, but it was fun.'

Her voice was a carefully modulated

instrument of encouragement. 'And?'

'I left them all. Don and Sam, Joe and Chandra. Evans — the lot of them.'

'Tell me about it,' she insisted.

'What is there to tell?' he shouted. 'I left them. Abandoned them on the frozen hell of Pluto and ran back to Earth. They trusted me and I betrayed them. My crew. The men who trusted me. Even good old Evans. He'd saved my life and thought of me as a son. Some son! I broke faith with him. Broke with all of them. I was their commander and I acted the coward. I deserted them. Ran away. Left them to die on the edge of the Big Dark!'

He fell silent, panting, the breath rasping in his throat. He wiped his face and looked at the sweat on his palm. His hands were trembling. 'So now you know,' he said quietly. 'That's the man you say you love. A dirty, stinking coward. A commander who abandoned his crew. There can be nothing lower.'

'Jules!'

'I can see them now,' he said dully, ignoring the woman. 'Don and Joe, Sam and Chandra. They stood there with

116

Evans pleading with me to save them. I can see them now, their faces pale against the black ice, the thin hydrogen wind tugging at their hair. Their mouths were open, gaping like the mouths of landed fish, and they reached out like children wanting a treat. I can see them just as they were, standing there outside the ship, pleading, begging.'

He drew a sobbing breath. 'Then I killed them,' he said. 'I fired the engines and left them to rot.'

Silently Illraya poured him the last of the wine using her own glass. 'Drink it,' she ordered. 'All of it.'

Dutifully he gulped the spiced coldness.

'We're making progress,' she said conversationally. 'Now you are able to remember the names of your crew and talk about them. You can even talk about how you left them. That is good.'

'For you, perhaps,' he said. 'As proof that your therapy is working. But not good for me. I can do without that knowledge of the past. Or do you think I should be proud of having deserted my men?'

117

She was enigmatic. 'That rather depends.'

'On what?' he said sharply. 'You know now what I did.'

'No,' she corrected. 'We know what you think you did and that is demonstrably untrue. You keep saying that you left your crew to rot,' she explained. 'You couldn't have done. When you fired the engines, your blast must have burned them to ash. Death would have been instantaneous.'

'And that makes a difference?'

'I think it does.'

He shrugged, unwilling to argue. 'I killed them,' he said. 'How doesn't matter.'

'No,' she admitted. 'The 'how' isn't so important. But the 'why' is. Why did you do it, Jules? That's what we must discover. Why did you abandon your crew? Why?'

Neither of them heard the opening of the door.

7

Change of command

It was Brensco and he was drunk.

Incredibly the cold, ice-minded man of science was intoxicated. He swayed and leaned against the edge of the door. The heavy gun in his hand wavered as he tried to hold it steady, fell to his side as he forgot his original intention. He parted thin lips in an idiotic grin as he looked at Illraya.

'Happy?'

'I'm perfectly well, thank you, Captain,' she said evenly.

Brensco snorted. 'That's not what I asked you,' he said. 'I want to know if you're happy.' He grinned as he lurched into the room.

Illraya watched him as she would a cobra.

'Answer me, woman!'

'I think you had better leave,' she said

emotionlessly. 'You need sleep and rest. Let me give you something to drink.'

'No.' He lunged towards her, the gun swinging wide as he opened his arms. 'I'm the captain, remember? You are supposed to do everything I say. If you don't, then it's mutiny and I can shoot you down.' He sucked his thin lips. 'Mutiny,' he said thickly. 'Shoot you down like I did the others. Kill you before you can kill me. Are you one of them?'

'No, Paul,' she said. 'Of course not.'

'They're everywhere,' he said in a whisper. 'Watching me all the time. They want to take over my ship. They want to kill me because they know I am the most important man in the world. I rule like a god. My orders have to be obeyed without question. Shall I tell you something? I am a god! I live among the stars. That's why they hate me. That's why I have to kill them before they can kill me.'

'Yes, Paul,' she soothed. 'But you don't have to kill me.'

'No,' he said. 'I don't have to do that. Give me a kiss.' She hesitated and his face darkened with rage. 'You heard me,' he snapped. 'Obey!'

'Paul, why don't you let me get you a drink?'

He frowned and the gun in his hand snapped up level with her waist. If he pulled the trigger, the blast of flame would burn her to a crisp. Slowly he tensed his finger as his eyes searched her face.

'You're an enemy,' he said. 'I thought you were a friend, but you've failed the test. You're one of those against me. I've got to kill you! Kill you!'

Carmodine slipped from the therapy couch. In one coordinated movement he snatched the gun from Brensco's hand and shoved the captain back against the bulkhead. 'Get a hypo,' he snapped to the woman. 'Something to knock him out.'

Brensco straightened, rested his shoulders against the bulkhead at his rear and, with the force of a released spring, threw himself at Carmodine. His extended fingers clawed at the eyes, the stiffened edge of the palm of the other hand chopped savagely at the throat. As he

121

moved, his knee exploded upwards toward the groin.

Carmodine sprang to one side and slammed the barrel of the gun against the side of Brensco's head. Somberly he looked down at the unconscious figure of the captain.

'He broke,' said Illraya, and shuddered. 'Did you see his eyes? Alcohol on top of the various drugs he's been taking was enough to send him over the edge. He was on the verge of running amok. If you hadn't snatched the gun, he would have burned us all.'

'Crazy,' said Carmodine. 'I never thought to see Paul like this.' He drew a deep breath and straightened his shoulders. 'Dope him,' he ordered. 'Keep him under. Give him what treatment you can to get him back to normal.'

He stepped from the room into the corridor outside. A man, pale with tension, stood against the wall some distance down the passage. He was young, newly commissioned, and this was probably his first exploratory flight. He stepped forward as he saw Carmodine.

'The captain, sir,' he said. 'Is he . . . ?'

'Out,' snapped Carmodine. 'Flat on his back with a head full of dreams.'

'He's a sick man, sir,' said the youngster. 'I've been following him about the ship in case something happened. I . . .' He broke off, swallowing, out of his depth. 'I didn't know what to do,' he confessed. 'We're almost within orbitting distance of Pluto and I've been waiting for orders.'

'Pluto?' Carmodine glanced within the room. Brensco was still sprawled on the floor, relaxed now that Illraya had given him injected sedatives, the harsh lines of fear and suspicion erased from his features. 'Give me a hand,' snapped Carmodine to the officer. 'Help me get the captain on the therapy couch.'

Brensco was surprisingly light. He had obviously been fasting, probably afraid to eat for fear of poison and using stimulating drugs to give himself energy. 'Where are the other officers?'

'Confined to quarters, sir. The captain imagined they were plotting to take over his command.'

'Were they?' Carmodine stared at the young man, then shrugged. 'Never mind that now. Release them immediately. Tell them to meet me in Control.'

'Yes, sir.' The youngster hesitated. 'Sir,' he blurted. 'How long will the captain be unconscious? We're close to our destination and we haven't got an astrogator. Both the first and second pilot were killed in the action, sir.'

Carmodine frowned. 'Who's left?'

'Mason, sir, the first engineer, Kerlen, his second; Winguard, in charge of hydroponics and me, sir, Trainee Electro technician Turman.'

'I see,' said Carmodine musingly. Then, sharply, 'You have your orders, Mr. Turman. All officers to report to Control immediately. Move!'

'Sir!'

Carmodine smiled as the young man snapped a salute and raced off on his errand. It was good to use the words of command again, taste the heady power of being obeyed. But the young officer was reacting to ingrained discipline. The officers would be able to think for themselves.

In the control room, He looked at them. Mason was no problem, but the others were unknown quantities. Curtly he explained the situation.

'The captain is unconscious and unable to retain command of the ship. As an emergency measure, one of you must take over. I understand that we are approaching our destination and soon will have to swing into orbit. Your astrogators are dead. Can any of you navigate the vessel?'

Mason shook his head. 'I can plot a rough course with the aid of the computer,' he said. 'Make a landing if I have to, but I can't do that and tend the engines at the same time.'

'Your second?'

Kerlen shrugged. Like Turman, he was a Trainee still needing to learn his trade. 'I'll do what I can, sir,' he said formally. 'But if anything goes wrong, I may not be able to handle it.'

'Winguard?'

'If you want to keep breathing, you'd better leave me where I am,' said the grizzled hydroponics officer. 'I'm tending the place and I know how to do it. If I try to land this crate, I'm liable to make a mess of it. I'm all right if there's a landing beacon from down below, but out here . . . ?' He shook his head. 'Sorry, Carmodine. I guess it's up to you.'

'We've talked it over,' said Mason quickly, before Carmodine could protest. 'After I left you with Doctor Samorova, the captain ordered me to join the others in their quarters. He locked us in. It was natural to discuss what was going to happen. Well, it's happened. We need you. You can't let us down.'

Carmodine looked from one to the other. 'Do you know what you're asking?'

'We've no choice,' said Mason. 'Not that it makes any difference, but you're the only one aboard who can get us down in one piece. Even if the captain were still on his feet, we'd rather you take over the command. You didn't see him when he was walking the ship with a gun in his hand, ready to let fly at shadows.' He glanced at the others. 'As the total officer strength, we have the right to remove the command from a captain we have reason to believe is unsuitable. We offer you the

126

command on unanimous agreement. Do you agree to accept it?'

Carmodine hesitated, and then said slowly, 'Yes, on one condition. The crew must agree to obey my commands.'

Mason made an impatient gesture. 'Why?'

Winguard blew out his cheeks. 'It'll take time,' he said slowly. 'We're pretty near rendezvous point. Unless we want to overshoot and head directly into the Big Dark, we'd better do something about manoeuvering the ship.' He turned to Turman, snapped an order. 'Release the men. Get them up here for Captain's Assembly. Go with him, Kerlen. Take guns but don't wave them about, and use them only if you have to. Even then, aim to miss, not to burn. Move!'

He turned to face Carmodine as the two junior officers raced down the passage. 'We'd better get busy. Mason can handle trim and I can relay from the computer.' He looked past Carmodine's shoulder at the flight panel. Flashing coloured lights reflected from his eyes, a scatter of miniature stars. His expression changed to one of horror. 'God!' he said. 'Dear God, don't let it happen!'

Carmodine turned, ran his eyes over the instruments then ran to the captain's chair. Ahead of them, a dark circle occluding the stars, waited the ebon bulk of the frigid world.

'The pulse!' yelled Mason as he ran to his station. 'Those mutineers blasted us off course when they fired the rockets. We're aimed straight at Pluto!'

'What'll we do?' asked Winguard, and then, mastering his panic, 'Computer ready for your orders, captain.'

'Trim in position, sir,' echoed Mason.

They were none too soon. Theoretically it was possible for one man to operate the ship. Automatic relays made takeoff a matter of pressing buttons on preset controls. During the journey, the essential life-support apparatus would function without human intervention. Only when the voyage was long and the complement large was it necessary to oversee routines. But landing was a different matter.

In the inner worlds, a single-man ship could be landed by planet-based control.

Landing beacons would guide the ship down by remote control. Pilots could be sent up to join an orbitting vessel. Help was always at hand. But on the edge of the Big Dark there was no one to help. No planet-based computers. Out here, a ship landed unaided. Only a very special type of man could hope to do it on his own.

Carmodine checked the instruments. The apparent diameter of the planet gave its distance. The swelling of that diameter gave visual indication of the velocity of the vessel. Radar added to the information. Figures were processed by the computer and answers calculated almost instantly. Winguard, sweating, checked and correlated, refed the equations into the machine and checked the answers. Out here, there could be no mistakes. Any error was an automatic death sentence.

'Spin ship,' snapped Carmodine. 'One hundred and seventy-three degrees right. Mark!'

Gyroscopes whined as they spun into shimmering life. Slowly the ship turned opposite to the spin of their motion, not wholly about-face. Carmodine had no intention of allowing the planet to roll past so that he would have to come to a relative halt and then waste fuel chasing their target.

Mason called from the trim panel. 'One hundred seventy-five. Mark!'

Carmodine stabbed the warning siren.

'Hear this,' he called as the wail died into silence. 'Jets about to fire full for thirty seconds, followed by one-tenth. Take acceleration precautions.' He glanced at the engineer. 'Gravity compensators.'

'Adjusted, sir.'

Carmodine felt himself lighten as the gravity plates in the deck were adjusted to a weak pull while those in the ceiling were activated. He waited, watching the swing of a hand across a dial.

'Five,' he said into the microphone. 'Mark!'

He felt the jerk, the rolling vibratory thunder of the venturis as they blasted their energy against the hull. Despite the gravity compensators, he felt the weight of deceleration. It eased as the initial high-thrust ended and the compensators restored normal gravity.

He checked the instruments and rose from his chair. 'Everything's under control now. Let's talk to the crew.'

They waited outside the control room, a battered group of men, many with crude bandages covering ugly burns. The two junior officers stood at the rear, self-importantly, guns visible in their hands.

'Give me those.' Carmodine took the weapons and handed them to Mason, who put them in the control room, out of sight.

'Now listen,' said Carmodine to the men. 'Things have happened aboard this ship which should never have occurred, but we aren't going to talk about the past. Brensco is no longer your captain. His command has been taken from him by the full complement of officers and acting officers. They have offered it to me. They appear to be satisfied, but officers alone do not make a happy ship. The men are just as important. I do not intend to force you to accept my discipline.'

He paused, looking at them, his face

reflecting his bitterness.

'I am a criminal,' he said abruptly. 'I was delivered to this vessel in chains. My life is forfeit for a crime no man could forgive. I commanded the first expedition to Pluto and I abandoned my men. I left them to die. They trusted me and I let them down. I tell you this because I want you to decide. Do you want me as your captain?'

The silence grew as they stared at him, digested his words, arrived at their decision.

A man stepped forward. He had a stained bandage around the upper part of his left arm. 'I'll take you rather than Brensco any time,' he said curtly. 'That scut burned us down without warning. Would you have done that?'

'No,' admitted Carmodine. 'But I have done worse. You must remember that.'

'I'm remembering it,' said another man. He was tall with a bald patch at the side of his head where a blast had seared his scalp. 'But I'm wondering why you told us about it. Are you afraid to land on Pluto?' He craned forward, eyes shrewd.

'What's down there? What's waiting for us?'

'I don't know,' admitted Carmodine. 'But we don't have to land at all. We can go back now. I'm giving you that chance.'

'Wait a minute,' said the man, who leaned against the wall of the passage. 'Let's get this straight. You'll be our captain if we agree, right?'

Carmodine nodded.

'And you'll take us back home if we want to go?'

'Yes.'

'So you're giving us free choice?' The man looked at his mates. 'What do you say, lads? We've come a long way to return empty-handed. We've got a mutiny to account for and the League won't be gentle. If we go back without taking a look at what we've come to explore, they won't be willing to give us a chance and never mind what the Federation says. But if we do go down, discover something of value maybe, and if the captain backs us and we back him . . . well . . . who can tell?' He grinned with a flash of teeth. 'I say we follow Carmodine down to Pluto.'

They chorused their agreement.

'Hold it,' said the man with the bald patch. 'What about Brensco?'

'He's ill,' said Carmodine quickly. 'Under therapy.'

'He should be dead,' snapped the man. He touched the side of his head. 'He damn near took an ear off when he came shooting into the engine room. I'd like to give him a taste of what he gave us. Tie him up and focus a laser at his feet.'

'That's enough of that talk!' Carmodine glared at the man, eyes cold, mouth a vicious line. 'The past is dead. Let it go. I'm your captain now and don't forget it. You'll do as I say or, by God, you'll regret it. Now get back to your duties. Those of you who are injured, report to the therapy room for treatment. The rest of you, resume your normal stations. Move!'

He felt Mason at his side. 'You've got the touch,' said the engineer. 'Men don't mind a firm commander if he's fair. In fact, they prefer it. The trouble with Brensco was that he made the mistake of thinking that firmness and harshness were the same thing.'

The engineer hesitated. 'When are you going to land, Captain?'

'Soon.'

'When will that be?' Mason was insistent. 'I've got to be at the engines when you begin to make the long drop. Kerlen, too. What are we going to find down there?'

'Ice,' said Carmodine. 'Frozen gases, mostly. There might be a little free hydrogen. No liquids unless there is some liquid helium around. We didn't find any the last time I was here.'

'What else, Captain?'

Carmodine met the engineer's eyes.

Mason was hard, determined. 'You've got to do it, sir,' he said. 'You're the captain now. You've got to accept your responsibility. If for no other reason that you are now in command of men, you have to remember what it was you met down there. But,' he added slowly, 'I think there is a better reason than that. You owe it to yourself.'

'And to the woman?'

'You know that better than I do, sir,' said Mason stolidly. 'But, if it were me she was in love with, and this thing stood between us, I'd walk barefooted into Hell to get rid of it.'

All Carmodine had to do was walk to the therapy room.

8

Alien life

The light spun and sparkled, sending little flashes of brilliance into his eyes, lulling with its regular pattern of darting motes. Carmodine rested on the therapy couch, the pneumatic cushions moulding to his body, his head supported so that he could look into the light without physical strain. Illraya stood beside him, together with Mason.

The engineer moved restlessly.

'Are you certain you need me here?' he asked. 'There's work I could be doing. The engines — '

' — will not be used for landing unless we can clear the captain's mental blockage,' interrupted Illraya sharply. 'Please don't be negative. You want the expedition to be a success, and you want Jules to fill in the missing portion of his memory.' She smiled, the warmth of her expression taking the sting from her reproof. 'And you are a friend,' she reminded. 'As such, you are a valuable ally.'

She pushed the hair from her eyes, adjusting the golden fillet that kept it in place.

'You know what we are doing,' she said quietly. 'The use of hypnotism is somewhat primitive but, even in this day and age, it can be extremely effective. The one essential, full cooperation of the subject, we now have. Until Jules really wanted to regain his memory, we could only attack it from the edges, as it were. We fought a continuous battle in which ground was only yielded after a struggle. Even so, the nexus of the problem remains. We must find out what made him wish to forget.'

'Something nasty,' suggested Mason. 'Something too bad to be remembered.'

'Possibly, but not necessarily so,' said Illraya. 'Memory is the characteristic of living organisms in virtue of what they experience leaving behind effects which modify future experiences and behaviour. That characteristic underlies all learning, the essential feature of which is retention . . . in a narrow sense, it covers recall and recognition. This we call remembering. Now Jules is suffering from amnesia, which is an inability to remember. This can be total or partial. His amnesia is localized; that is, it is restricted to a special time and place, but complicated by also being retroactive. The inability is extended to events immediately preceding a trauma.

'The problem is to bring to the surface those events so that we may learn what the shock really was. The task has been made unnecessarily difficult by the careless use of psychoprobes, which have driven the incident even deeper into the subconscious. However, the therapy has been so far successful in that he can now think of his crew, the journey and other basically irrelevant matters without suffering automatic psychosomatic withdrawal symptoms.'

She smiled at the engineer. 'Are you able to follow?'

'I think so,' said Mason slowly. 'Up until now, if you mentioned something he wanted to forget he'd show physical signs of distress. Get an ache, maybe, or a pain, or even black out if you pressed too hard.'

'Exactly.' Illraya picked up a hypogun from a tray and checked the setting. 'The light has thrown Jules into a superficial hypnotic trance. He can hear what we say and is fully conscious, but he is so comfortable that nothing can easily bother him. This is a first-stage trance and serves mostly to relax the subject. Quite often it is only necessary to deepen the trance to effect a complete scan of the subject's complete life. However, where there are complications, this treatment is ineffective unless much time and skill are devoted to it. So we shall use drugs to achieve a deep trance together with complete cooperation of the subject.'

She aimed the hypogun at Carmodine's arm and pressed the trigger. The blast of air that spat from the instrument carried the drug through clothing and skin into the bloodstream. Putting down the hypogun, she adjusted the light.

'Relax,' she murmured softly. 'Allow yourself to sink into the light. It is like a tunnel into which you are travelling. You see the walls pass all around you as you go deeper and deeper. And, as you progress, so you become more and more relaxed.'

She caught Mason's intent expression. 'The verbal commands are really unnecessary at this stage, but may serve to emphasise the previous instructions. In a few moments, when the drug has had time to act, I shall give him a specific direction in which to travel.'

'Backwards,' said Mason. 'Back through time to the period of the first expedition.'

Illraya nodded and stooped over Carmodine. 'Close your eyes,' she ordered and gently lowered his lids. 'You are floating in a soft and wonderful cloud,' she murmured. 'You have no fear and will have none. You are immune to all danger. Nothing can harm you. You can travel anywhere you wish. The place you really would like to see is a spot you have been to before. To reach it, you must go back through time.' Her voice hardened a little. 'You are going back to when you were young. Back to when you graduated. Tell me about it.'

He stirred a little but remained silent.

'Tell me of what you see,' she insisted. 'You are graduating. Where are you?'

'In the great hall of the university,' he said. 'There are a lot of us. We are waiting. I am very happy.'

'Move forward,' she commanded. 'You have received your first command. You are coming in to land at Luna Station. Tell me the procedure.'

'Check velocity,' he murmured. 'Contact base for permission to land. Cross-couple ship and base computers for remote control. Check all stations. Board showing total green. Go!'

'You are older,' said Illraya. 'You are in a ship hanging on its lower jets over the Great Red Spot of Jupiter. There is a storm. Your engineer Evans is with you.'

Carmodine jerked as if to the thrust of rockets. His face contorted as sweat oozed on his forehead. His hands clenched, the muscles bunching in his arms. His voice was strained, harsh as he spoke to the remembered engineer, waited for an answer, spoke again.

To him, the therapy room had changed,

become the confines of a ship's control room, swayed and jerked to the pound of storm and flaring tubes.

Time passed and Carmodine fell silent. Illraya sighed and glanced at the other man.

'Ideally this procedure should be spread over several weeks, but we simply haven't the time. I'm going to bring him right up to the time of his first landing on Pluto. He may show signs of violent strain. If he does, I want you to restrain him. I wouldn't be strong enough to do it alone.'

Mason nodded, running his tongue over dry lips.

Illraya paused, and then, with sudden decision, spoke to the man on the couch.

'Jules, you are about to land on Pluto. You are in command of the first expedition and are about to land. Tell me about it.'

His voice was clear and unstrained. 'I am approaching on course. Orbitting, scanning the planet, routine landing procedure. Radar shows a flat plain at the north pole; a place ringed with mountains. I have decided to land on the plain.'

His voice droned on and the listeners could imagine the smooth activity in the vessel, the mounting excitement as they neared the mysterious world. Mason could almost smell the scent of the engine rooms, the ozone, the strange odours that he liked to think of as being the stench of burnt atoms. He glanced at the woman, opened his mouth to ask a question and closed it again at her fierce gesture.

'We have landed,' said Carmodine evenly, and fell silent.

'You have landed,' said Illraya. 'You have sent out an exploratory party. What did they discover?'

'Nothing unexpected. Frozen gases. Traces of minerals.'

Illraya frowned, thinking.

'You are on the plain,' she said, and this time used the present tense. 'You are with the field party. What have they found?'

'No,' he said. 'Don't ask me that.'

'You must answer,' she insisted. 'Tell me. What have you found?'

'Crystals,' he muttered. 'Strange things of ice, but they do not melt. Pretty things. So beautiful that a man could wear one for a jewel. So beautiful . . . ' His voice trailed into silence.

'Tell me of the crystals, Jules.'

'No!'

'Tell me!'

He shook his head, teeth gritted, blood showing where they had bitten into his lips. Blankly, Illraya looked at the engineer and then at Carmodine on the couch.

'He's fighting,' she said. 'Tearing himself apart in order not to answer.' She spoke directly into his ear. 'Jules, you are about to leave Pluto. Tell me of that.'

He shook his head.

'You have told me before,' she reminded. 'How you sat at the controls. You are looking into the visiplate and just about to fire the tubes. What do you see?'

'Evans!' he screamed, writhing on the couch and lunging to his feet. Mason caught him, sweating with the effort, and managed to force him back against the cushions.

'No!' Carmodine jerked against the engineer's restraining hands. 'They're all there. Evans and Joe and Sam and Don and Chandra. All of them. I mustn't leave them. I can't, and yet . . . '

'They are dead,' said Illraya sharply. 'All your friends are dead.'

Carmodine groaned. 'Dead?'

'What else? Look at them,' she ordered. 'Their pale faces, the thin wind ruffling their hair. They aren't wearing their suits are they Jules? They aren't wearing any protection at all. And yet they are on an airless world!'

Carmodine's throat worked as if he were choking on a word. 'Dead?'

'Yes, Jules. Something killed them. What was that thing? What is it that has twisted your mind so that you can't answer? What is the mystery of Pluto?'

She fired the questions like bullets and each made an impact. Carmodine shuddered and his mouth worked and emitted small, weird noises like those a child would make before it has learned to talk — or a grown man makes when he has forgotten how. Quickly Illraya picked up the hypogun and blasted a sedative into his blood.

'You will sleep now,' she ordered. 'Sleep

and rest. You will remember everything when you wake and I shall tell you when this will be. You will remember everything that has happened, but it has lost all power to hurt you now. It can never hurt you again. You will sleep now. Sleep.'

When he woke, he was sane.

'It was a common mental blockage,' said Illraya. She handed him a cup of the coffee she had made while he was sleeping, handed another to Mason and picked up her own. 'You had lost a portion of your memory relevant to the mysterious crystals you spoke about. Something tampered with your mind and, without that essential reference, you could only believe one thing: all the available evidence went to convince you that you had deserted your companions.'

Illraya sipped her steaming coffee.

'The guilt complex was more than you could tolerate, and so you tried to escape by denying to yourself what had really happened. Instead, you built a false explanation that was logical in that it both accounted for the available evidence and gave you justification for self-punishment.

Neat, but then the mind works that way. It is always perfectly logical if you can once grasp the premise on which it is working.

'I gained the first clue as to what must have really happened when you spoke of seeing those men without their suits as you fired the engines. Obviously they must have been dead then. Equally obviously, something must have given you the impression that they were still alive. What was it?'

He frowned. 'I can't remember.'

'Yes you can, Jules. You can remember everything now. Stop running when there is no need to hide. What made you leave those men?'

'They were dead,' he said slowly. 'Worse than dead. And there was danger. I had to get away.'

'Why?'

Carmodine frowned, his features creasing as he strove to arouse the dormant portion of his mind.

Illraya stared at him, eyes snapping with impatience.

'Listen,' she said urgently, 'You spoke

of finding some crystals. You said they were pretty things. So beautiful that a man might wear one for a jewel. What made you say that? Men aren't in the habit of wearing jewels. Women, yes, but not men. Is that important? Did some danger lie in those crystals?'

'I'm not sure,' he said slowly.

'Then what of the men you thought you'd abandoned? You imagine them to be alive, calling to you, pleading to be rescued. Yet how could that be? They were without suits on an airless world. How could you hear sounds?'

'That's right,' said Mason. He had been quietly listening to the exchange. 'Sound doesn't travel in a vacuum. How about it, Captain?'

Carmodine shook his head. 'I don't know,' he admitted. 'I don't know about the crystals either. I know we found them, but that's all. But I'm sure about the men. I heard them calling to me.'

Illraya was sharp. 'You're positive about that?'

'Yes,' said Carmodine. 'I saw them. Their mouths were open and their hands

149

reaching out. They were begging me to take them with me. Damn it!' he exploded. 'I know! I was there! I heard them!'

Mason frowned and cleared his throat. 'If you did,' he said, 'as far as I can see, there can be only one explanation. You certainly didn't hear actual voices because that would have been impossible.'

'Telepathy.' Illraya looked thoughtfully at the engineer. 'Of course, Mason! It must have been that. Emitted thought directed at Jules. He mentally translated it into normal terms, and so was convinced he heard voices. It makes perfectly logical sense.' White teeth gleamed as she bit her lower lip. 'You realise what this must mean?'

'Alien life,' said Mason slowly. 'But out here, at the edge of the Big Dark? On Pluto?'

'Alien life wouldn't have to follow the same survival patterns as those we know,' said Illraya. 'It is perfectly reasonable to accept the fact that there are living intelligences on the planet below us. From the evidence we have, it seems that

150

it is able to control men's bodies. It is also telepathic and, for some reason, badly wanted to enter the ship.'

'To be carried to the inner worlds,' said Carmodine. 'To the habitations of men. Somehow they managed to erase the knowledge of their presence from my mind. But why should they have done that?'

'I can think of a reason,' said Mason grimly. 'They didn't want us to know about them. To be warned of what they are. We still don't know what they are or what they look like, but we can guess one thing — they aren't friendly. For me, that's enough.'

'Yet we have to land,' said Illraya. 'We have no choice. We have to find out what is waiting down there.'

Carmodine made no comment. There was no need. They all knew what waited on the frigid planet below.

Alien life that had already killed five men.

9

The beautiful crystal

The ship fell on spouting fingers of blue-white fire, plummeting to the dark, star-limned surface of the frigid world, checking and scanning with powerful searchlights and sweeping curtains of radar.

They droned over the irregular surface, split and marred by gigantic crevasses and craters, covered with the compressed bulk of frozen gases. They swung high over the mountains surrounding the north pole, then, as the radar showed a relatively smooth area among the saw-toothed peaks, they checked, balanced and gently lowered themselves to the surface of the night-shrouded plain.

Carmodine relaxed, letting himself sink deep into the snug comfort of the captain's chair. With a skeleton crew, the landing had not been easy. Mason came up from the engine room. He glanced at Carmodine, then at Winguard, finally at Illraya, who had been impressed to watch the screens.

'Anything?'

'No,' said the woman. 'Nothing remotely resembling artifacts as we know them. No houses, roads, cultivated patches. No signs of activity. No lights. No movement of vehicles of any kind. Nothing. The entire planet seems to be nothing but a frozen ball of matter.'

'Nothing on the radio either,' said Winguard. 'I've been covering the entire electromagnetic spectrum, and if anyone had been transmitting on any waveband, I'd have spotted it.'

'How about direct-beam transmission via laser?' asked Mason. 'Or there could be vibratory communication through the crust.'

Winguard was sarcastic. 'Sure. And they could have had a line of insects transmitting via antennae. Or invisible men using invisible semaphores. There are a lot of ways they could communicate if they wanted to. That's assuming there is anyone down there who wants to send messages in the first place. If you ask me, the whole planet is just one giant ice cube. The only life possible would maybe be a few drifting spores or a surface virus. Stuff that's come down from space itself.'

'Yes,' said Mason. 'I guess you're right.' Winguard hadn't been told of what the others knew. 'Unless you missed something, of course.'

'Naturally,' snapped Winguard. 'Have I ever claimed to be infallible?' He glanced at Carmodine. 'With your permission, Captain? I'd like to get back to the air plant.'

Carmodine nodded. 'Go ahead.'

'Thank you, sir. Any instructions?'

'No. I'll be addressing the crew myself shortly.' Carmodine stared at the screens as Winguard left the control room. His eyes were thoughtful, sombre. 'We must have landed very close to here the last time,' he said quietly. 'The area is too small to allow for much variation. We could probably find the old traces if we looked for them. We might even find — '

'No,' interrupted Illraya. 'Your crew

isn't out there. You burned them to ash. Remember?'

Carmodine nodded, eyes on the screens. It was cold out there with the utter chill of close to Absolute Zero. Bodies would last indefinitely in such a temperature. Dead men would lie as if sleeping, their blood ruby ice within their veins, their flesh iron-hard, their eyes frozen into glassy marbles.

But there was no one out there. No bodies lying on the frigid plain. He had seen to that with the searing incandescence of his blast at take-off.

There could be no dead, accusing eyes.

'Jules,' said Illraya. 'Jules!'

He turned and smiled at her. 'I'm all right,' he said. 'Just thinking.'

'You said that you would address the men,' she reminded. 'They are waiting.'

Had he sat brooding so long? Leaning forward, he thumbed the intercom button. 'Hear this,' he said. 'We have made a successful landing on Pluto and we have a lot of hard work ahead of us. But not now. Now we rest and eat and sleep and take things easy. Later we'll settle down to work. Have fun.'

He relaxed as Illraya came to stand at the side of his chair. Silently she opened the speaker-circuit. They could hear the sounds of the crew. Laughter, easy talk, jokes and good-natured horseplay. A man struck up a song and others joined him. Within seconds, the ship echoed to the roar of powerful voices. Carmodine listened for a moment, then took the woman's hand from the switch. At the same time, he activated the automatic screens that would signal the approach of any object.

The roar of song echoed through the control cabin as the men pressed into the recreation quarters, busy with cards, games, personal items.

'They sound happy,' said Illraya. 'That's good.'

'Yes,' said Carmodine. 'Let them enjoy themselves while they can.'

Some captains would call it bad discipline. Some commanders would have had the men stand watch, don suits and make outside patrols, sleep close to their guns and eat at action stations. Some officers would have stuck to the rule book and played it safe. Carmodine knew better.

He knew how the dull, grinding monotony of a long spaceflight could sap morale. He realized how nerves could be overstrained, tightened to a pitch where men fired at shadows, filled the days with alarm. The crew would be better for a rest, a chance to relax and amuse themselves. Later would come the hard work and hard discipline, but now they had the bitter taste of mutiny to wash from their memories.

It was wise to let them relax while they had the chance.

But, for him, there could be no rest.

'Go and join the others,' he said to Mason. 'Ask Winguard to let you have some of his liquor. If he says he hasn't any, then he's a liar. I've never met a hydroponics man yet who didn't have a ferment going somewhere.'

'Thank you, Captain.' The engineer paused at the door. 'And you, sir?'

'I'll stay here,' said Carmodine. 'I've got some thinking to do.' He felt the touch of Illraya's hand as she stroked his hair. 'They're out there,' he said. 'Somewhere in the dark. Buried in the ice, perhaps, lurking in some fissure, high on the sides of the mountains. But watching. If there is anything out there at all, they must have seen us land. They could be coming toward us this very moment.'

'They can't get in,' she soothed. 'If they get too close, the screens will warn us.'

'If they are of a material the screens can detect,' he pointed out. 'A gas could get past. A cloud. A mist or fog.'

'A trickle of fluid seeping over the ground,' she added. 'A convection current. A scrap of raw energy. But what if they can? Nothing immaterial can penetrate our hull.'

'Nothing we know,' he corrected. 'And we don't know what is out there. But having the men on watch won't give us added security. And neither will you losing your sleep,' he added. He lifted his hand and caught her delicate fingers. 'Get some rest, Illraya. That is, if you can ignore that noise they call singing.'

'I can,' she said. 'And it's a sound I like to hear. Men who sing like that aren't plotting mutiny.'

She kissed him and was gone.

Alone, Carmodine settled into his chair and stared broodingly at the screens. Outside, the mountains on the plain reflected the light of stars in their coverings of ice so that the scene seemed to shimmer and become unreal, the mountains to rear up into the heavens, to flatten and join with the plain.

A trick of the light. Eye-fatigue, the mind tending to fit inappropriate images on barely seen detail. He blinked and then suddenly tensed, lunging forward in his chair, brows furrowed, heart thudding painfully against his ribs. For a moment, he imagined that he'd seen something moving on the frozen wastes. A tall, man-like shape, striding across the plain, others behind the first, a line of figures marching towards the ship.

He drew a shuddering breath and forced himself to relax.

It was inconceivable that men could exist unprotected in that frigid hell. They couldn't be out there. Evans. Don and Joe, Sam and Chandra, were all scattered ash blowing in the thin hydrogen wind. His eyes were playing tricks again, his tired brain supplying shapes of nightmare.

Sighing, he settled back in the snug confines of the chair to stand his lonely watch.

He was dozing when Mason entered the control room. The engineer carried a steaming cup of coffee. He put it down on the arm of the chair and shook Carmodine by the shoulder.

Immediately he was fully alert. 'Trouble?'

'Far from it. The men have had their fun and are itching to go. I thought it would be best to have one party under Winguard and one under me. Does that meet your approval, sir?'

'It does,' said Carmodine. Gratefully he sipped the hot coffee. 'Send Winguard out first,' he decided. 'Have him do a quick scout in the immediate vicinity of the vessel. Warn him and the others about bringing anything back with them. Especially tell them, under no circumstances, to return with anything looking like an ice crystal or jewel.'

'The things you found before?' Mason frowned. 'Have you remembered — '

'No,' interrupted Carmodine. 'But I don't intend to take any chances. Get that party off. I'll wash up and come down later.'

'Right,' said Mason. He hesitated. 'One other thing, sir. Brensco wants to see you. Doctor Samorova had him put in one of the cabins. I took him some food and he asked after you.'

Carmodine finished his coffee. He felt rested and guessed that he must have fallen asleep without knowing it. He felt Mason staring at him.

'About Brensco, sir?'

'You think I should see him, don't you?' Carmodine put down his empty cup. 'Well, let's go.'

Brensco looked up from where he sat on the edge of a bunk as they entered the locked cabin. His face was ravaged as if by internal stress, but his eyes had lost their insane brightness. He rose as he saw Carmodine, taking one step forward before halting with an obvious effort. He looked at his clenched hands and slowly opened his fingers.

'You wanted to see me, Paul,' said Carmodine.

'That's right.' Brensco looked at Mason, then at Carmodine. 'I want to know what is going to happen to me,' he said. 'If I am to be kept a prisoner by you mutineers, then — '

'One moment,' snapped Carmodine, interrupting. 'Let's get the situation clear. You are not the victim of a mutiny. You have been ill. Your officers were forced to relieve you of your command so that you could have appropriate therapy.' He paused. 'They offered me the command, Paul. I accepted it. I am now the captain of this vessel.'

'You!'

'That's right,' said Carmodine steadily. 'Odd isn't it? A prisoner and I end up being the commander. Well, life can be like that.'

'Yes,' said Brensco tightly. 'But the game isn't over yet Jules. You are not going to steal my command if I can help it. I'm not going to have you desert my men as you did your own!'

Carmodine stiffened. 'I'm not going to argue with you, Paul. Why did you want to see me?'

'Isn't it obvious? I want to get out of here. I want to move about the ship, go outside, collect samples. You might be in temporary command, Jules, but this is still my expedition and I want to make it a success.' Brensco made an effort to control his temper. 'I am a scientist,' he said in a quieter tone. 'I am also officially in charge of this expedition. You had your chance, Jules, and you wasted your opportunity. This is my chance. Are you going to waste it, too?'

Mason coughed and shifted his feet. Carmodine stared at the engineer.

'Do you think he should have the run of the ship?'

'That is up to you, sir,' said the engineer. 'Doctor Samorova did say that he was cured of his delusion. I asked her before I woke you,' he explained. 'Shall I fetch her, Captain?'

'It doesn't matter,' said Carmodine. He

163

looked at Brensco. 'We're short-handed. I can't spare anyone to stand guard over you. If I allow you the run of the ship, will you promise to cause no trouble?'

Brensco almost choked. 'Promise? You?'

'I'm waiting, Paul,' said Carmodine patiently. 'I will admit that I'd rather not keep you confined if it can be avoided. But unless you give me your word, I have no choice.' He waited, and then, with sudden irritation, turned towards the door. 'We can't waste time here,' he said to Mason. 'There is too much to do.'

'Wait!' Brensco stepped forward and caught at the edge of the panel. 'I'll be allowed outside? To take samples?'

Carmodine nodded. 'Your word?'

'You have it,' said Brensco. And then, viciously, 'It should be good enough. Have you ever known me to lie?'

'No,' admitted Carmodine. 'I haven't.'

He turned and walked from the cabin, Mason at his side. After them came Brensco, a king deposed, but one who was unlikely to either forget or forgive.

The first party to venture outside circled the ship within sight range. They

164

checked the temperature of the surface, the air, took sightings on selected stars so as to determine the exact rotation period of the planet. The second party went as far as the mountains and brought back samples of rock, ice and frozen snow.

Brensco went out with the third party and brought back a shimmering crystal.

It was a thing of breath-stopping beauty, a radiant gem catching and reflecting the light in a myriad of shining points, countless facets burning with prismatic colour and scintillating brilliance, an elfin crown of delicate tracery and enigmatic construction. He held it in his gloved hand, its eye-catching glory filling his palm, radiance spilling from his fingers as he moved the gem to catch the light.

The men of his party crowded around him in the vestibule of the airlock. They still wore their suits, but they had opened their helmets and their eyes were wide as they drank in the incredible beauty of the strange crystal Brensco had found.

Others joined them, attracted by the mysterious power of rumour. The off-watch men, the on-watch, Winguard, the two junior officers, Mason. They stared and they marvelled. They looked and wondered.

It was too beautiful.

It was the sort of thing that a man would give his soul to possess and a woman would give that and everything else she could call her own, everything she could get. It presented the ultimate in man's eternal search for beauty. A shimmering, twinkling, ever-changing, ever-different crystal of supreme magnificence.

'I want one,' whispered one of the men. 'Are there more?'

'Lots more,' said Brensco.

'Enough for all of us?' Kerlen moved a little closer.

'There are enough to give us all as many as we want,' said Brensco. 'Enough to fill the ship.'

'Think of what one of those things would fetch back home,' said a man. 'They'd pay a fortune for it. With just one of those, a man could live easy for the rest of his life.'

'If you had one, would you sell it?'

Winguard thrust himself forward and drank in the scintillating beauty. His eyes were hot, feverish. 'Man! I want one of those!'

He voiced the general thought of everyone present.

They wanted them to look at, to touch, to wear as a jewel. They wanted more to sell. An insane lust of possessive desire gripped them as they looked at the crystal. It spelled more than simple beauty. It spelled riches, power, comfort, everything they had ever wanted in a shape that could be held in the palm of one hand.

Brensco watched them with blue, calculating eyes. Of them all, he seemed the least affected by what he had found outside in the frozen snow. He stood just within the vestibule of the airlock, his helmet framing his thin features and blond hair. A man waiting.

He hadn't long to wait.

Carmodine came running from the control room, thrusting his way into the cluster of men, eyes blazing as he snapped orders. 'Watch crew, get back to your positions. Off-watchmen, clear the air-lock. Winguard! Mason! Get some order here. Move!'

He glared at the field party. 'Why are you still in suits? Where are your samples? Damn it, you all know better than to clog the deck like this. Brensco, what the hell is this all about?'

Brensco twisted his lips in a smile as he faced the big man. As if by accident, his free hand brushed against the butt of the gun he wore in an outside holster. Carmodine glared at him, then jerked men from his path as he lunged forward.

'Brensco! What the devil is this? What . . . '

He saw the crystal.

He looked at it, staring at the shimmering glory with eyes that widened into pools of midnight blackness. He gulped, sweat streaming from his fore-head over his contorted face, his hands, his whole body trembling to a violent reaction of tearing emotion.

'The crystals,' he whispered. 'No. No!'

His hand was a blur as it darted towards the holstered weapon at Brensco's side.

He jerked it free, lifted it, smashed the heavy barrel hard against the man's wrist. The crystal spun from Brensco's palm, a shimmering splendour as it landed on the floor, lights winking from it as Carmodine aimed the gun.

Fire blasted from the weapon. A searing bolt of incandescent energy, thundering as it sheared the air, raw energy making the men cringe backwards away from the savage heat. The bolt blazed downwards to sear the deck.

And blasted the crystal to splintered dust!

10

Brensco's gambit

For a long moment there was silence as the rolling thunder of the gun died in fading echoes. Then a man cried out in shocked anger.

'He burned it!'

Another joined in. 'Destroyed it!'

'It's gone!'

'Smashed to dust!'

'Silence!' Carmodine glared at the assembled men. He spun to face Brensco and the blond man fell back, his hand fumbling with his empty holster. 'You gave me your word,' he said. 'Is this how you keep it?'

'What are you talking about, Jules?' Brensco had recovered his composure. 'What trouble have I caused? I merely brought a specimen to the ship. An unusual crystal I found at the foot of the mountains. What was wrong about that?'

'I warned you,' snapped Carmodine. 'I warned everyone not to touch anything like that they might find. I told everyone that, under no circumstances, must a crystal be introduced into the vessel.'

'No,' said Brensco. 'You didn't tell me. And what would it matter if you did?' His eyes lifted from Carmodine's face, drifted over the watching men. 'In any case, why issue such an order? Would it be because you wanted to keep all the crystals for yourself?'

'What!'

'You are a self-confessed criminal,' said Brensco coldly. 'Could it be that you secretly intended to load the ship with the crystals? They would be worth a tremendous fortune on the inner worlds. A fortune large enough to satisfy the greed of any man.' His voice thickened. 'More than enough to console him for having abandoned his crew.'

'You lying swine!'

'No, Jules. It's no lie. Have I learned the reason for your lost crew? Killed, abandoned for the sake of what you could make? They needn't have died, Jules.

Surely there was enough for you all. Or does your murderous greed accept no limitations?'

Carmodine stepped forward and smashed his fist through the open faceplate of Brensco's helmet. The blond man staggered back, blood on his mouth, his blue eyes glazed with hate.

'It's true, isn't it?' He spat a mouthful of blood. 'What harm can there be in the crystals?' he demanded. 'Why shouldn't we have them if we want? Are you setting yourself up as the ruler of Pluto? Do you own the planet?'

'No,' snapped Carmodine. The gun in his hand jerked as he fought to control his temper. 'I don't own Pluto. The planet has its own life.' He stared at the sullen faces of the men. 'I tell you these crystals aren't what they seem. They are dangerous. More dangerous than you can guess, and not only to you, but to the people of the inner worlds.'

'Listen to him,' Brensco sneered as he looked at the sullen faces. 'What does he think we are? Children? You all saw the crystal. It was a harmless piece of natural formation and was probably made of an unknown isotope. It was a beautiful thing and others like it could make us all rich. Is there any harm in that?'

'Carmodine was here before,' said a man slowly. 'Maybe he knows what he's talking about.'

'He does,' said Mason. 'You can take it from me.' He glared at his trainee engineer. 'Come on, Kerlen. We've got work to do.'

'But Mr. Mason, I . . . '

'Are you disobeying an order, Mr. Kerlen?' Mason smiled grimly. 'I thought not. Then, if you would be so good as to get to the engine room, I'll describe the inner maintenance of an Efertharm converter. Move!'

Winguard cleared his throat. 'I should be attending the plant,' he muttered. Brensco shrugged as he left.

'They don't seem to be interested,' he said to the others. 'Maybe they don't have to be.' His eyes searched out the man who had commented. 'It's true that Carmodine was here before and we all know what happened. He returned alone.

He wrecked his ship and tried to hide. Why? Can you think of a reason? I can.'

His eyes stared coldly at the captain. 'Let us assume that he collected some of the crystals. He didn't want to share with his crew, so he abandoned them. But landing a ship is hard work for one man alone. He made a mistake and crashed it in the Grosso. Then he tried to hide in Crater 4. He lived with freaks. That's the kind of man who is stopping you all from enjoying a fortune.'

'You lie,' said Carmodine thickly. 'Now shut your mouth before I smash in your face.'

'He doesn't want me to tell you all this,' said Brensco quickly to the watching men. 'He wants to load up the ship while you're all off-watch. When he's ready, he'll think of some excuse to get us all outside so that he can leave us behind. How would you like to stand out there on the plain watching the fire of his exhaust grow small in the sky? To know you're going to die when your air runs out? To watch him run for home and all the comforts money can buy? Your money!

Running off to spend it. Him and that red-headed bitch of his!'

'Leave Illraya out of this.' Carmodine's voice was very quiet and dangerous.

'Why?' Brensco demanded. 'Is she too good for us? Did you plan all the details together while she had you on that couch of hers?'

Carmodine poised the gun in his hand. 'All right, Paul,' he snapped. 'You asked for this.' He lunged forward, the heavy weapon swinging in a savage arc towards Brensco's head.

The helmet saved Brensco. He reeled back, hands lifted as Carmodine dropped the gun and sent his clenched fist slamming against the blond man's nose.

He turned in time to meet the concerted rush of the others. They piled on him, shouting as they carried him to the floor. Carmodine struck out, feeling the jar as his fists hammered against flesh and bone, oblivious to the punishment he received in return.

Brensco, his face a mask of blood from his broken nose, stepped forward, eyes cruel as he stared at the helpless man.

'All right, Jules,' he said mockingly, 'Now it's my turn.'

He swung his foot and sent the heavy boot slamming against Carmodine's temple. He kicked again as the big man slumped into unconsciousness, the metal-shod sole gouging deep into his side. He kicked again, this time at the ribs.

'Hold it!' One of the crewmen had picked up the gun. He aimed it casually at Brensco. 'There's no need for that. Kick him again and I'll burn your legs off.'

'He destroyed the crystal, didn't he?' Brensco glared his fury at the man with the gun. 'He intended to run off and abandon us all.'

'Maybe, but there's still no need to kick his ribs in.' The crewman jerked his head at a couple of others. 'Take him to the therapy room and have the woman take care of him. Hurry back. We're going after more of those gems.' He looked at Brensco. 'You're going to guide us,' he said flatly. 'Show us where you found the one you had. And just in case you're tempted to get clever, just remember that I've got this gun.' He hefted the weapon.

'And don't think I won't us it if I have to. I haven't forgotten how you treat a mutiny.'

'I was ill,' said Brensco. 'The woman gave me poison under the guise of treatment. She and Carmodine intended to take over the ship all along.'

It was a good lie and could possibly have been true. Brensco pressed his advantage. 'Come on,' he urged. 'Let's get those gems. Just think of how much they'll be worth on the open market.'

He had them. Like children, they raced to get into their suits, standing impatiently as they cycled through the airlock, gathering in a compact crowd outside on the frozen plain.

In the therapy room Carmodine groaned and opened his eyes. He sat upright, wincing as pain stabbed his chest, probing his ribs as he searched for damage.

'Nothing's broken,' said Illraya coming through the door. 'I've checked. You're bruised, but fortunately that's all.'

Carmodine grunted. His head ached and every breath was painful. 'What happened?'

'Brensco kicked you around a little. Then a couple of the crew brought you in here.'

'Where are they?'

'The men? All outside with Brensco.' Illraya crossed the room to a cabinet, opened it and took out a hypogun. 'They even made Mason and his junior go with them. We're the only ones in the vessel.' She aimed the instrument at the side of his neck. 'I'll shoot in something to ease the pain. There's not much else I can do.' Her finger closed on the trigger. 'Better?'

He flexed his arm and the muscles of his chest and sighed with relief.

She replaced the instrument in the cabinet. 'What's this all about, Jules? The men who carried you in here said something about going outside to collect some crystals. You spoke about crystals before. The same ones?'

Carmodine nodded.

'You found them on your first trip,' she urged. 'You seemed to be afraid of them.'

'With reason. Those crystals are instruments of the Devil. That's why I ordered everyone to leave them alone. I didn't want some fool bringing one back for a souvenir.' He frowned, black brows ridging across his eyes. 'I reckoned without Brensco.'

'He fetched one inside?'

'He did,' said Carmodine grimly. 'I think he did it deliberately. He wanted to set the men against me and regain control of the ship. Like a fool, I did and said all the wrong things and practically gave him what he was after. Now he's got the whip hand.' He paused, thoughtful. 'Or he thinks he has,' he said slowly.

'He's made a mistake,' said Illraya quickly. 'What is it?'

'Brensco is outside with all the crew. After the performance he put on, he couldn't avoid it, and that's his big mistake.' Carmodine slid from the couch and headed towards the door. 'They are out and we are inside the ship. Can you use a gun?'

'If I have to.' Illraya followed him out into the corridor. 'Why?'

'You may have to shoot someone,' he said curtly. 'Threaten them, at least.' He halted, looking down at her as she stood at his side. 'Brensco's mistake is our one big opportunity. We can seal all ports aside from the main entry, override the emergency controls so they cannot be opened from outside. That means the men will be stuck out on the plain. Them and their damned crystals. We'll have them on toast.'

Illraya frowned. 'I don't get it,' she complained.

Carmodine was impatient. 'I'm going up to one of the turrets. You'll be standing inside the inner door of the main airlock. I'll let the men in one at a time. You search them as they enter and make sure they haven't any crystals hidden away. Then you lock them in one of the storerooms. You could even use your hypogun to drug them unconscious. The main thing is we'll have them where we want them. Brensco and the others can be out on the ice. But we've got to hurry. They might already be on their way back.

Ten minutes later Carmodine sat in one of the turrets. He had a radio unit with him and settled down in the padded firing seat staring through the transparent canopy at the dark mystery of the frozen plain.

It was warm in the turret. Tiny signal lamps glowed as he checked the weapon hung in swivels in an airtight compartment beneath his part of the blister. A spot of light moved against the transparency as he adjusted the sights, died as he threw the controls back to inoperative standby. There was no point in wasting power.

Outside the cold stars wheeled across the ebon sky. Out there lay the Big Dark, the awesome space between the Sun and the nearest star, almost four light years of aching emptiness. But, one day, men would cross it as they had crossed the first ocean. The same courage that had sent them from the comforting sight of land would see to that. Across oceans, across interplanetary space to far-flung Pluto, and then across interstellar space to Proxima Centauri, the nearest star. And later? The yawning gulf of intergalactic space itself, perhaps. Who could tell?

Carmodine stiffened as, far on the plain, a spot of light flashed like a temporary star.

It flashed again, throwing a circular patch of light on the plain, bobbing and weaving as it came towards the ship. Others joined it, a host of tiny lights flashing and gleaming far below. Carmodine stared at them and his hands drifted over the controls of the turret. Instruments told that the gun was now war-operational. As the advancing lights came close, he pressed a button.

A miniature sun flared from the skin of the vessel as a searchlight flared into life. A hard, white circle of brilliance shone on the plain below and, on that circle, Carmodine trained the sight-bore of the turret gun.

Abruptly the radio broke into life. 'Hello, the ship. What gives?'

'Stay where you are!' Carmodine rested his hand on the firing release of the gun. A spear of artificial lightning lanced from the muzzle and steam boiled upwards from where it seared the plain.

'Are you crazy?' The voice from the radio was thin with strain. 'That damn blast almost fried me to ash! What gives in there?'

'Shut up and listen,' snapped Carmodine. 'What's your name?'

The man was sullen. 'Fenshaw. What's all this about, anyway? Who the hell are you?'

'Carmodine. Now step into the circle of light.'

'Why?'

'You've got a choice,' said Carmodine patiently. 'You do as I say or you stay where you are. If you hope to get inside the ship, you'd better do exactly as I say.' His voice became brittle, sharp with command. 'Now move!'

Slowly, Fenshaw stepped into the circle of radiance. His breathing sounded harsh, strained, as it came over the radio. 'What now?'

'Dump those crystals you're carrying.'

'What?'

'Is something wrong with you, mister?' snapped Carmodine. 'Are you deaf? You heard what I said clear enough. Now dump that junk and be quick about it!' He raised the muzzle of the gun and sent a blast of energy across the plain. On the distant mountain, a spot glowed as it received the impact of the shot. 'I'm not playing, Fenshaw. Now get rid of that rubbish.'

Sullenly, the man threw several scraps of shimmering beauty to the ground.

'Right. Now move onto the airlock. When the outer door opens, step into the vestibule. If you've got a gun, lay it on the floor. Stand with your hands raised above your head and make sure they are empty. You'll be searched inside, so don't try anything. If you cause trouble, I'll leave you out here to rot.' He raised his voice a little. 'Did the rest of you hear that? I want each man to do exactly the same thing.'

He listened to the sudden babble of voices from the radio. The men were incoherent in their anger. They fell silent as he fired the turret gun for the third time. The blaze of the shot illuminated the plain with painful brilliance. The following darkness was deeper by comparison.

'Now I suggest you stop talking and get on with it,' said Carmodine evenly. 'You stay where you are until you've gotten rid of those crystals. I'm not having that filth on board my ship.'

It hurt, but they had no choice but to

obey. Carmodine relaxed a little as a man stepped into the patch of light and reluctantly threw down his crystals before moving towards the airlock.

Carmodine reached out and pressed a button. 'Illraya?'

'Yes, Jules.'

'A change of plan. Don't let anyone in until I give the word.'

'As you say, Jules.'

Carmodine relaxed a little more. Let them stay outside until they had gotten rid of what they carried. He would order Mason to be the first through the lock. The engineer would make a welcome ally, unless he also had become contaminated with the crystal-mania. Even so, he and Illraya could manage better than the girl on her own. He must have been stupid not to think of it earlier.

Outside, one of the space-suited figures sagged as if in distress.

'Jules.' The voice was thin, panting. 'Jules, this is Paul.'

Carmodine narrowed his eyes. 'What is it?'

'You've got to let me into the ship,

Jules.' The panting echoed louder. 'For God's sake, Jules.'

'You'll have to wait,' said Carmodine. 'I don't trust you, Paul.'

'I can't wait.' Brensco sounded desperate. 'I forgot to recharge my air tanks. I'm dying, Jules. Dying!'

'All right,' snapped Carmodine. 'But get rid of your crystals first. Hurry.'

Brensco staggered into the circle of light, threw down some crystals and swayed as if about to fall. Over the radio came the stomach-squeezing sounds of a man retching for air.

'Two of you men help him,' ordered Carmodine. 'You, Fenshaw, and the man behind you. Quick! Get him into the lock. Put him down and get back outside.' He pressed the button of the intercom. 'Illraya?'

'Yes, Jules?'

'Open the outer door.'

'Okay.'

Carmodine released the button and stared at the assembled men. Carefully, he aimed the gun, adjusting the setting back to the original low power.

'All right,' he snapped at the radio. 'The rest of you get back. Stand well clear of those crystals.'

Deliberately he blasted the little heap of shining beauty to scattered ruin, then, leaving the turret, ran down to where Illraya waited at the lock.

She turned at his approach. 'Something wrong, Jules?'

'Paul's in the lock. He's run out of air. Said he was dying and sounded like it, too.' He spun the control that sealed the outer door and commenced the recycling process. Air began to gush into the vestibule. 'He might be lying, but we can't take a chance.'

She nodded, understanding. As a doctor life, to her, was a precious thing. 'What of the others?'

'They're still outside. It won't hurt them to wait. This is an emergency.'

A lamp flashed green over the inner door as the cycle reached completion. Carmodine spun the locking wheel and swung open the door. Inside the vestibule, a suited figure lay sprawled on the floor.

187

'He's alone anyway,' said Carmodine. 'You stand well back and keep your gun aimed at him. If Paul is bluffing, we'll call it. If he isn't, he should be unconscious by now. We'll know as soon as I open his helmet.'

'Be careful,' said Illraya.

'I will,' said Carmodine.

He entered the vestibule and dropped to his knees beside the silent figure. He pulled, rolling Brensco over on his back. Through the faceplate, he could see the bruised features of the blond man. His eyes were closed, his breathing unnoticeable. Carmodine moved a little closer, his hands gripping the helmet release. With a jerk, he opened the helmet.

'How is he, Jules?' Illraya had moved to stand in the inner door of the vestibule. 'Does he need medical attention?'

'Stay well back,' ordered Carmodine. He squinted at the helmet instruments but couldn't make out the gauges. They were designed to be read from within the helmet, not from outside. He reached out and lifted the lid of one eye, seeing only the veined white of the ball. 'He seems to

188

be unconscious,' he said.

He moved, crouching over the figure, leaning forward to touch the throat. The pulse was strong, regular.

Too strong!

He jerked back a fraction too late. Something smashed viciously into his groin and blossomed into a hell of pain. He retched, tasting bile, doubled and rolling in helpless agony.

'Jules!'

'Drop the gun!' shouted Brensco. 'Drop it!'

'Jules!' Illraya was sobbing. 'I can't shoot, Jules! You're too close!'

Carmodine writhed as he felt steel-tipped fingers claw at his face, reach for his eyes.

'Drop the gun!' ordered Brensco harshly. 'Now! Before I tear out his eyes!'

11

Parasite

The storeroom was small and badly ventilated from a single grill. A solitary light threw a weak illumination over the gleaming metal of walls and bulkheads.

The door was closed and locked by an electronic device. Carmodine kicked it and paced back across the floor. He limped a little and his face was savage.

'Tricked,' he said. 'A schoolboy would have had better sense. It wasn't even as if I trusted him! I knew Paul would try something if given the chance.' He kicked the door again, turned and resumed his pacing. 'The oldest trick in the book and I had to fall for it.'

'You couldn't help it,' said Illraya. She sat on the deck, back against the bulkhead and her long legs stretched out before her. 'You did what had to be done.'

'I should have burned him down while

I had the chance.' Carmodine halted, glowering. 'At least I should have taken better precautions. He fooled me,' he admitted. 'Rolling up his eyes so as to pretend he was unconscious. Waiting until I was in exactly the right position and then giving me his knee. Threatening to blind me unless you gave him the gun. The swine!'

'He's changed,' she admitted. 'I warned you that he would. Now he is totally dedicated to his own ambition. Finding the crystals seems to have made him worse.' She paused, thinking. 'What are they, Jules? Why are you so afraid of them? The crystals, I mean. They seem harmless enough.'

'Harmless?' He laughed without humour. 'Yes, Illraya, they're harmless enough. As harmless as a lethal virus or a primed atomic missile.'

'But they're so beautiful,' she protested. 'Any woman would give anything for one. I'd like one myself.'

'You've seen them,' he said sharply. 'When?'

'After the fight. Brensco threw you in here and made me help operate the lock.

After a few men had passed through, he didn't need me, but I saw the crystals. Jules, they're lovely. Can something so beautiful be so dangerous?'

Carmodine stepped forward, stooped over the woman, gripped her soft shoulders until she winced with pain.

'Listen,' he said tersely. 'Don't ever let yourself be fooled by mere appearances. A cobra is a beautiful thing — but it can kill. Fire is beautiful and you know what fire can do. The radioactive elements have an eerie beauty when seen in the dark, but you know what unshielded radiation can do. Illraya, those crystals are as deadly as they are beautiful. Make no mistake about that.'

'But in what way, Jules?'

He released her and stepped back. She rose, eyes thoughtful as she saw his strained expression.

'Tell me, Jules! You know! Tell me!'

'They are alive,' he said, and his eyes grew wide as he stared at her, at her and past her into some previous time. 'Alien life, a strange crystalline form of awareness. They are quiescent as the current is in an uncoupled battery. A complex mesh of electronic sub-etheric stress, individual wave-patterns locked in the crystals, potential entities in a form of stasis that could be eternal. But they are a form of alien life following rules of survival peculiar to themselves.'

'Alive,' she said slowly. 'Those crystals? It doesn't seem possible.'

'We found them on the first expedition,' said Carmodine. He lifted a hand and rubbed his temples. 'The first few hours after we landed, I began to fully remember. Sight of that crystal Brensco brought with him into the ship brought it all back. They're alive, Illraya, as I know only too well.'

He paused, remembering. 'We had landed. After the preliminary survey, we went out in pairs to collect samples and Chandra and Sam found some of the crystals. Naturally we were all excited at the discovery. They were beautiful and seemed as if they would have a high intrinsic value. We felt exactly as Brensco and the others feel now, so we kept the crystals.'

Illraya stepped quietly before him. 'And?'

'They were dormant life,' he said. 'Alien life. Even now I can't do more than guess at what must have happened. Something must have triggered them into operating awareness. I don't know just what, but I suspect that it might be the emanations of normal thought. Our brains are electrical in nature and the things may have been able to receive the broadcast wave-pattern of that activity, low though it must be. Maybe it was the residual radiation from the engines or something as simple as our own body heat. It happened. They became fully aware. The life in the crystals woke and sent us all to hell.'

He paused again and sweat shone on the taut muscles and planes of his face.

'I told you we kept them. Why not? They were beautiful and seemed harmless. Just an unusual crystal that seemed to hold brilliant rainbows. Evans loved them. He wore one as a jewel.'

'An alien product?' Illraya frowned. 'Could he have been so foolish?'

'We'd done our best to test them,' said Carmodine. 'Raised their temperature, checked for radiation, tested them for spores, all the usual things. As far as we could tell, they were just what they seemed . . . interestingly shaped pieces of crystal. Anyway, Evans threaded a thong through a couple of openings in a crystal and wore it around his neck like a medallion. To stop it swinging when he stooped, he tucked it inside his blouse. I think the others may have followed his example. Certainly we had all claimed one of the gems as our own. But I know Evans wore his touching his bare skin.'

'I see,' said Illraya thoughtfully. 'You probably wouldn't have tested for the acid reaction caused by human perspiration, body heat, static electricity and cellular aura. Wearing one could have triggered it off.'

'I know that now,' said Carmodine. 'I didn't then. As far as I was concerned, Evans had suddenly changed. I was off-watch at the time. I'd gone to sleep watching the play of colours over the crystal I'd placed beside my bunk. I'd been dreaming and I woke to find Evans stooping over me. He'd taken my crystal and had placed it on my bare chest. I sat up and it fell off. He tried to replace it and then I noticed his eyes.'

'They weren't human,' said Illraya.

Carmodine stared at her, gripped her by the shoulders. 'How did you know?'

'I guessed.' Deliberately she drew away from him, hands lifted as she rearranged her hair. The curves of her body were taut against her blouse. 'You forget that I've had experiences with alien life forms from Mars and the gas giant satellites, and that you were under deep hypnosis during questioning. I couldn't be certain then, but if your friends could live and move, appear to scream and plead while in an almost total vacuum, then obviously they could no longer be men as we know them. They must have been inhuman.'

'You're right,' said Carmodine grimly. 'Whatever lies in those crystals has the power of robbing a man of his personality. Evans still wore his crystal and I saw it as he stooped over my bunk. It had changed. The colours had gone, the brilliance. It was just a piece of dead stone. The life it had contained had moved and taken over the mind and body of a man.'

Illraya drew in her breath. 'Evans.'

Carmodine nodded, then held up his hand for silence. Someone was treading heavily down the passage outside the storeroom. The footsteps halted and something pressed against the door. Obviously satisfied the panel was firmly locked, the man moved on.

Carmodine crossed to the door and rested his ear against the metal. He listened, then shook his head.

'Nothing. My bet is that everyone is cooperating with Brensco to the full. I'd hoped that Mason at least would have had the sense to stay sane.'

'Maybe he has,' suggested Illraya. 'But he'll have to wait for his opportunity to help us.' She sat down again. 'You were telling me about Evans.'

'That's right,' said Carmodine. 'I pushed him away. The thing inside him must have realized that I'd sensed something was wrong, but he tried to convince me otherwise. He was full of plans as to how we could load the ship with crystals and take them to the inner worlds. He kept telling me how rich we would all be, how powerful and, all the time he was talking, he kept trying to rest the crystal against my bare skin.

'I resisted, naturally. If I hadn't, I wouldn't be here now. I pushed Evans away and got up and dressed. He stood and watched me all the time, and still he kept on and on about the ship, the gems, how pretty they were and how important it was that we should take them back with us. I knew that it couldn't be Evans talking, because he would never have kept on like that, but I also knew that I had to be careful. I made him a half-promise, which seemed to satisfy him, and then went in search of the others. They were all the same as Evans. The crystals had taken over everyone but me.'

'You were lucky,' she said. 'How did you get away?'

'More luck. I knew that if I once showed suspicion or tried to go against them, they would overpower me. I agreed that we should load up with the crystals and suggested they go collect them while I checked the ship. I hoped to separate them, getting each man alone and stripping him of his crystal. I never had the chance.

'They went outside. They walked like robots to the airlock, squeezed in, shut the inner door and opened the outer. They were in too much of a hurry that they forgot to wear suits. Maybe they just didn't realize what the suits were, but whatever it was in those crystals didn't realize the external environment would be fatal to men. They learned fast enough. They knew they'd made a mistake when the air gushed from their lungs and their blood began to boil through lack of pressure before it froze. That's when they dropped all pretence and began to plead with me to take them back into the ship. I could see them through the visiplate. It was as if they couldn't understand what was happening to them or, if they did, realizing it too late.'

Carmodine drew a deep breath, hunching his shoulders as if to shed an oppressive burden. 'That's about all there is to it. I knew that I couldn't save them, that they were not still human, but they wore the faces of old friends. I had no choice but to take off. I crushed the remaining crystals when the ship had reached optimum velocity. When I did that, something must have happened to my mind. All I could remember was that I'd abandoned my crew and hated myself because of it.'

'Obviously something in the crystals you smashed must have blanked out your memory,' said Illraya thoughtfully. She rose and paced the floor. 'The rest was protective amnesia. Hating yourself, you tried to punish yourself for what you had imagined you had done. Then you simply lost memory of the entire incident — an expansion of the protective forgetfulness.' She frowned. 'It's odd that Paul didn't discover that totally blank area when he used the psycho probes. Maybe — ' She broke off as heavy footsteps sounded again in the passage. They halted beyond the door. 'Jules?'

'No,' he said curtly. 'We take no chances until we know what we're going up against.' He stopped back as the door opened.

Brensco entered the room.

He stared at them from his bruised features. He was naked to the waist and around his neck hung one of the crystals. It was suspended from a thong and looked like a dull fragment of glass. The blond man's eyes were those of a stranger. Cold chips of blue ice stared at the woman and Carmodine. Glass marbles like those used as toys by the very young. They held nothing resembling emotion. No hate. No rancor. No bitterness. Not even curiosity.

It was that which made Illraya feel a mounting inner tension. It was like being stared at by a snake. By something so alien that its very thought processes were utterly incomprehensible to the normal world. She cringed as he looked at her, trying to press her body through the steel bulkhead.

'Paul, please don't look at me like that.'

Brensco looked from her to Carmodine.

'I have brought you something.'

He threw two of the crystals to the deck. They lay, shimmering with exquisite

201

beauty, and each crystal had been threaded on a thong. 'You will each wear one as I do. Hang the thong around your neck so that the crystal lies against your skin. You will do this immediately.'

'Paul,' said Illraya, 'Don't make us do this — '

Brensco stared at her with his blank eyes. 'Why do you object? Is what I am asking so terrible? They are beautiful, are they not? What harm can lie in things so lovely? Wear them!'

'And if we refuse?' asked Carmodine.

'I regret the necessity,' said Brensco evenly, 'but it is essential that there should be skin contact with the containers. It takes a certain amount of time for full empathy to be obtained between host and entity. You will assist matters by cooperating. If you do not, then I will have you immobilized for the necessary period.'

It wasn't Paul speaking, not the man he had grown up with, fought with, ridden across the long, empty miles to this bleak planet with. This was a stranger, and worse than that. An alien stared from

202

those blue eyes and spoke with that flat voice.

'You admit it, then,' said Carmodine. 'You are an alien life form which has taken over the body of a man.'

'I am an intelligence using the body of a host,' said Brensco's voice.

'A parasite!' Carmodine felt muscles ridge along the line of his jaw. 'And if you expect us to wear those things against our skin so that others of your kind can move into our minds and bodies, you know what you can do? You can go straight to Hell!'

'Jules!'

'Keep out of this,' snapped Carmodine. He didn't look at the girl. 'What does he think we are? Cattle to be ordered around? If he thinks I'm going to let some dirty parasite use my body, then he needs to think again.'

Carmodine stepped forward to where the Brensco-alien stood, apparently a man consumed with anger, every vestige of his rage concentrated on the other man. But his eyes darted past Brensco's body, searched the corridor beyond the doorway and saw the pair of armed crewmen standing outside. Like Brensco's body they too wore dead lumps of crystal around their necks.

'Why?' Carmodine demanded. 'You've got the others. Why do you need us?'

The Brensco-alien lifted a hand, rested it against Carmodine's chest and pushed. His strength was incredible.

Illraya screamed as Carmodine slammed back against the far bulkhead.

'Jules!'

'I'm all right.' Dazed, Carmodine shook his head. The alien was using Brensco's body to the fullest extent, something no normal human ever did unless in a situation of supreme emergency. To do otherwise was to invite ligaments and bones to be torn and broken by the sheer power of ungoverned muscular contraction.

The Brensco-alien looked coldly from one to the other. 'I have learned from this rudimentary mind that creatures of your species are easily influenced by pain. It is a thing that you apparently fear. Later I will experiment with this concept on the envelope I wear. But for now, I will merely use the fear of pain to overcome your resistance to yielding your opposition.'

He stepped back and gestured to one of the men standing outside. 'I will give you one last opportunity to obey,' he said. 'If you continue to defy me, I shall order this man to fire at the legs of the female.'

Carmodine felt his nails dig into his palms. Brensco, or the thing which had taken over his body, would do exactly as he said. To him, Illraya was nothing more than an animal. Reluctantly, he stooped and picked up the pair of crystals. He handed one to Illraya and slipped the thong of the other around his neck.

'Against the skin,' said the Brensco-alien. 'It must lie touching the skin.'

Carmodine lifted the crystal and thrust it down the neck of his blouse. It rested, hard and glowing, against his chest. Illraya followed suit.

'You are acting with wisdom,' said the creature. 'You will now sit and wait for the transferrence to take place. You will not remove the containers. You will remain in this room, which will be locked.' The alien gestured towards the armed crewman. 'This person will wait with you. If you attempt to remove the containers, he will fire his weapon.'

He left and slammed shut the door.

12

Escape

Alone with the crewman, Carmodine and Illraya looked at each other.

'How long, Jules?' She looked down her blouse where the crystal hung between her breasts. 'It must be my imagination, but it seems to be getting warm.'

'It isn't getting warm,' Carmodine said curtly. 'And my guess is that the transfer won't take place for a while yet. If it happened quickly, the alien in Brensco would have waited until it was over.' He scowled at the armed man. 'Listen, you damned parasite! How long do we have to stay in here?'

'You will sit,' said the man woodenly. 'You will do as you were instructed. If you do not obey, I shall discharge this weapon and you will be injured.' He lifted the weapon as they parted to sit on opposite sides of the compartment. 'No. You will sit together. Side-by-side with your backs against the wall.'

This was no fool, thought Carmodine bitterly as he slumped down. At least the alien knew enough to make them sit where he could watch them both at once. Carmodine leaned back, looking at the man, acutely conscious of the weight of the crystal on his chest.

Even now an entity was waking in that gem. Becoming aware and getting itself ready to transfer that awareness to a new host. And what then?

Once the last two had been possessed by the alien life forms, there would be nothing to stop them from loading the ship with more crystals and leaving for the inner worlds. There would be no suspicion. Before the danger could be recognized, the parasites would be occupying the bodies of influential men and women. They would be in a position to rule the Homogenetic League, even the Federation. Mankind would become an endless source of new bodies for alien use.

'Jules,' said Illraya softly. 'We've got to do something.'

Carmodine stared at the guard and spoke without moving either his head or his lips. 'Jump him?'

'I don't know. But we can't let ourselves be turned into things like Paul's become without a struggle. Could you overpower the guard?'

Carmodine weighed his chances. Jumping the guard would be impossible. He leaned against the opposite wall a good twelve feet distant. Before either he or Illraya could get to their feet, the guard would cut them down.

'Don't look at me,' whispered Carmodine. 'We've got to get him over here. Pretend to faint or something. Once he's within reach, I'll do what I can.' He added quickly, 'Not yet. Give him a chance to settle down.'

He kept his eyes on the guard, willing him to meet his stare, to narrow his concentration. At his side, Illraya gave a groan.

Carmodine kept staring at the man with the gun.

'Please . . . ' Illraya lifted her hand, tore at the neck of her blouse and, as if by accident, pulled the crystal from where it had rested between her breasts. It still glowed with undiminished beauty. 'Ill,' muttered the woman. 'Feel . . . ill . . . '

'You will replace that container,' said the guard. He lifted the gun. 'Replace it immediately or you will be made to suffer.'

Carmodine turned, looked at Illraya and tucked his legs under him as he spun back to stare at the guard. 'Hold it. She isn't well. A fainting spell caused by overstrain and concern. Let me help her.'

'Stay where you are.' The guard's tone remained flat, emotionless. 'You will obey me,' he said to Illraya. 'Unless you restore that container to its previous position immediately, I will fire.'

Illraya moaned and fell to one side.

Carmodine felt his nerves crawl as the guard aimed the pistol. Carmodine moved towards Illraya and caught her shoulders. His body hiding what he did from the armed man, he jerked the thong hanging around her neck. It snapped and he grabbed the crystal in one big hand. Both hand and crystal were behind his back as he turned to face the guard once again.

'I've done it,' he said. 'I put the crystal back where it was, I mean.'

The guard looked at Illraya. Her mane of hair covered her throat and would have made the thong hard to see at the best of times. Sitting as she was, slumped, the hair spilled over her face, it was impossible to see if she wore the crystal or not.

The guard was thorough. He stepped forward to make certain.

Carmodine flung the crystal. It sliced through the air and tore at the guard's eye. He halted, raising the gun as he turned, his finger tightening on the trigger. Carmodine had thrown himself after the crystal. He gripped the man's arm, twisted and jerked the elbow hard against his chest. The joint snapped.

The guard made another attempt to lift the gun, but it fell from his limp fingers. Carmodine smashed his fist against the man's jaw and sent him reeling back. He stooped, snatched up the gun and, remembering Brensco's incredible strength, slammed the heavy weapon across the guard's skull.

Bone yielded.

Carmodine stood, breathing heavily as he looked down at the dead man. The guard had fallen face down and was lying in a widening pool of blood.

'Jules!' Illraya was on her feet. 'The crystal, Jules,' she reminded. ' 'Get rid of it!'

He lifted a hand and tore the thing from around his neck.

'The guard,' she said. 'Jules, is he . . . '

'I had to do it,' he interrupted. 'It was him or us — and he wasn't even human any more.' He stooped and gripped the dead man by the shoulder. He pulled and rolled him over on his back. 'Maybe he's got something we can use to get out of here. Maybe — '

He broke off, looking at the crystal that had hung around the dead man's neck. It was no longer a dull scrap of glass. Like the one Carmodine had discarded, it shone with a glowing splendour.

'Jules!'

He turned as the woman called. Footsteps sounded from beyond the door. Carmodine tensed, gun levelled as he faced the panel, then the footsteps moved on and he lowered the gun.

'We've got to get out of here,' he said, 'before Brensco gets back. I could kill him, but we wouldn't stand a chance against the others.' He fell to his knees and searched the clothes of the dead guard. Nothing. He scowled and ripped at the man's shirt, then paused as he spotted the belt. It was narrow and made of woven wire, soft and flexible. 'This should do it.'

'The belt?' Illraya was puzzled.

'It's self-made,' explained Carmodine. He handed her the gun. 'Most crewmen amuse themselves during the voyage by using their hands. These things were all the rage once. Thin, coloured and insulated wire, woven and plaited into various patterns, worn as a belt or lanyard or even as a neckband.' He tore at the end of the belt with his teeth. 'If I can get a strand free, the rest will be easy.' Again he ripped at the tough wire. Metal gleamed as he tore away the plastic insulation, then a strand ripped loose. He unravelled it, strong fingers gentle as he teased out the wire until he had a long piece free. He rose and examined the single glotube. 'The gun,' he said. 'Give it to me.'

Illraya handed him the weapon.

Carmodine rapped the barrel against the cover of the light. The blow made a thin ringing that echoed through the room. He tucked the gun into his waistband and ripped off his shirt. Wadding it, he held it over the cover of the light, grabbed the gun and slammed it down. Plastic shattered, falling as he lowered the shirt. He handed the gun back to Illraya, donned the shirt and picked up the wire. Eyes narrowed, he squinted at the light.

'I'm going to have to kill the light,' he said. 'Stand by the door and mark the lock. Ready?'

'Go ahead.'

He reached up with his strong fingers and wrenched the shining electric tube from its connections. Current stabbed his hand as he wrapped the stripped end of the thin wire around the terminal. Carefully, so as not to break the thin strand, he moved towards the door. He sensed Illraya's body heat, smelled the perfume of her hair as she stood in the sudden darkness.

He reached out with his free hand and touched the smooth curve of her hip.

'The lock,' he said. 'Guide me.'

She gripped his free hand, pulled it forward until it touched the door, downwards to where he had rested the barrel of the gun. A tiny hole pierced the panel, the gateway for an electronic key. Carmodine knelt, his free hand on the door just above the hole, the other hand moving the bared end of the wire towards the orifice.

Delicately he probed, blinking at sudden, tiny sparks.

'Got to be careful,' he whispered. 'These locks are just as liable to fuse solid as to open.' He probed again and gave a satisfied grunt as something clicked. 'Got it.'

He rose and felt Illraya by his side.

'The gun,' she said quietly. 'You had better take it.'

He felt the heavy weapon put into his hand. 'After we open the door,' she whispered. 'What then?'

'We work a bluff,' he said, and then, remembering, 'Get the thongs from those crystals. We'll wear just those. Unless we bump into Brensco, we might get away with it long enough to hit them before they can hit us.' He cracked the door a little, allowing the light from the passage to illuminate the room. He heard Illraya move behind him, felt her slip a thong around his neck and tuck the ends into the neck of his blouse.

'We need time to think,' she whispered. 'To plan. If we could get to the therapy room, there are things there that could help us. Drugs, anaesthetics, the hypo-gun . . .'

'You've got a plan?'

'I'm not sure,' she admitted. 'Just an idea, perhaps, but we can't do anything until we get out of this trap.'

'All right,' he said quietly. 'We'll make for the therapy room. If we run into trouble, leave me to handle it while you keep moving. Do it!' he snapped as she began to protest. 'One of us has to stay uncontaminated by these parasites.' He tensed. 'Ready?'

'Yes, Jules.'

'Then stay behind me, and remember, keep moving.'

He swung open the panel.

Outside the passage showed clear and deserted in the brilliant overhead lighting. Without hesitation Carmodine turned to his right and padded down the corridor. Luck was with them. Normally an alarm would have flashed at the killing of the glotube and the tampering with the lock. The alarm probably had flashed but no one had taken any notice.

Even if they had seen it the aliens might not know quite what it meant. They had taken over the bodies of their hosts and, apparently, could use the stored knowledge found in the brains of the humans, but it took time to fully identify.

Carmodine thought of the guard he had killed. The man had seemed to feel no pain. The blow from the crystal that had lacerated his eye would have ended the fight for any normal man. Even with a broken elbow he had tried to fire the gun. But he had been a little slow, a little

217

unsure, and Carmodine had taken full advantage of it. Like a driver, he thought. A man in an unfamiliar machine. He needed time to get used to the controls and to get the 'feel' of the vehicle.

The aliens must be in much the same position.

He halted at the end of the passage and looked down a connecting corridor. A man came towards him. He wore a thong around his neck and the bulge of a crystal could be seen beneath his shirt.

Carmodine stepped into the corridor as the man approached.

'These envelopes need fuel,' he said, facing Carmodine. 'One who has knowledge of how to prepare it is needed.'

'I am such a one,' said Carmodine. 'I will prepare the fuel.' He gestured at Illraya. 'This one also. It is our skill on this vessel.'

The man looked at Illraya. 'That one is a female,' he said slowly, as if searching a file for information. 'Females prepare fuel — no, food, for others. I can then leave the task to you?'

'Yes,' said Carmodine.

'I will then go and assist in other ways,' said the man. 'You will inform us when the fuel is ready for assimilation?'

'Yes,' said Carmodine. He released his breath in a long sigh as the man moved down the corridor. 'So far, so good. Let's get to the therapy room.'

They made it without further incident. Once inside, the door locked, Illraya yielded to reactive strain. Hands shaking, she spilled phials of drugs from the cabinet. 'Damn!' She glared at the mess.

'What are you looking for?' Carmodine checked the cabinet. 'Something for your nerves?'

'Yes.'

'Amphetamines will give you a boost,' he said, 'but they'll also distort your judgment by giving you an over-confident attitude.' He looked at a phial and put it aside. 'Tranquilizers won't help, either. What we could both use is a good measure of alcohol.'

'I've got some,' she said. 'Surgical spirit.'

'Couldn't be better.' He watched as she found a flask and two beakers. The spirit was chemically pure and almost evaporated in his mouth. His stomach signalled warm gratitude and he held out his beaker for more. 'You had a plan,' he said as she refilled his container. 'An idea. What is it?'

'Did you notice something about that guard you killed? The one in the storeroom,' she added.

'He was a little slow,' he said. 'And he wore a blouse, which Brensco didn't. I'm wondering why.'

'I think I know,' said Illraya. 'And I think you'll find that Paul will be wearing his blouse from now on. It is important to them to keep the crystals in contact with the skin. Paul must have wanted to show something to us, or perhaps it was his way of assuming leadership if they recognize any such thing. But I wasn't thinking of that, though it all ties in.'

He sipped his drink, waiting.

'When you killed that guard, his crystal suddenly regained its colour,' she said slowly. 'It became just like the one you'd thrown at him, and the one you had been wearing. All three looked exactly alike as regards the shimmering colours. I checked when I went to get the thongs.'

'So?'

'My guess is that whatever had taken that man over from the crystal had gone back when he died.'

'Back into the crystal?'

Illraya nodded. 'Yes. It's only a theory, I know, but it fits all the observed facts. And they call the crystals 'containers',' she added. 'Jules! Can you guess what this could mean?'

Carmodine looked down into his beaker. 'Immortality.'

'Perhaps not exactly that,' she demurred. 'But something so close to it as makes no difference. That's why I say Brensco will begin to wear his blouse. It makes it easier to maintain skin contact with the crystal. If the host is killed the body dies, but the alien intelligence goes back into the crystal from where it came.'

'You are assuming that actual contact is necessary for that,' he pointed out. 'That needn't be true.'

'Then why are they still wearing the crystals?' she demanded. 'If they aren't essential, then why not put them to one side? No, Jules. I swear I'm right in this. It gives us a chance, at least.'

He sat, brooding over what she had said. As things were the aliens couldn't even be threatened. They had no fear of pain or injury. But, if what Illraya had assumed was the truth it showed their weakness.

'We could separate them from their crystals,' he said thoughtfully. 'If they died, then they would have nowhere to go. It would be a real death. Those damned parasites wouldn't like that. We could kill them and regain the ship.' He paused and shook his head. 'No,' he said. 'Not kill them. If we did that, we'd be slaughtering the crew.'

'They aren't human any more, Jules. You said so yourself,' reminded Illraya. 'Not men as we know them.'

'Perhaps not, but their memories must be still alive,' said Carmodine. 'They have to be in order for the parasites to gain their knowledge. That's why they can talk in a language we understand. Use instruments they could never have seen before.' His big hand closed hard around the beaker. 'I've thought of that in the past,' he admitted. 'Wondered if somehow Evans and the rest hadn't been conscious in some way. Aware of what was happening. Like a horse that's being ridden over the edge of a cliff, knowing death lies beyond but helpless to do anything about it.'

'Jules!'

'It's true, isn't it?' he said fiercely. 'It has to be true. In each of those men out there is an alien, but there is more than that. Somewhere the original man is still alive!'

'No!' said Illraya sharply. 'It isn't necessarily true and you know it. The original ego, the individual, the man, could be totally obliterated and still leave all his memories intact. It happens in amnesia all the time,' she insisted. 'A man suddenly loses all memory of his past, but he still retains a knowledge of some skills. He can read and write, he knows how to walk and run, if he could swim before then he will still be able to swim. But the original man is, somehow, totally missing.

This could be a similar occurrence, Jules.'

'Could be,' he said bitterly. 'But you can't be sure. No one can.'

'That is true,' she admitted. 'But we have proof that the aliens do not completely take over all memories. Otherwise the first crew wouldn't have died in the vacuum. They must learn some things the hard way. As you must,' she added, suddenly impatient. 'Those things out there represent an awful danger to the inner worlds. Somehow we must prevent them leaving this planet. I shouldn't have to tell you what has to be done.'

He didn't answer, looking instead into the beaker and then abruptly throwing the container to one side. It was not an easy thing to face. No captain likes to abandon his crew. If he did what had to be done, Carmodine would be doing it for a second time.

'Your plan,' he said. 'I take it that you hope to knock out the crew in some way and remove the crystals. Is that correct?'

She nodded.

'We could use gas, I suppose. You have masks in here?'

'Yes,' said Illraya. 'But I was thinking of using hypoguns. We could get up close and shoot them full of dope.'

'And get ourselves shot while doing it,' he pointed out. 'Gas,' he said. 'Masks. If we could introduce it into the air system, it would be circulated all over the ship. With luck, they will fall before they guess something is wrong. We can remove their crystals and do what has to be done.'

She stepped before him and rested her hands on his shoulders. 'Say it,' she demanded. 'You can't afford the luxury of being gentle. They have to be killed. You know that.'

'Shot down,' he said. 'Driven outside without suits to die as Evans and the others died. Or did the things inside of them die?' He frowned, trying to remember. 'They would still have had their crystals.'

'You killed them,' she said. 'Burned them with your exhaust. They died right enough.'

'Yes,' he said heavily. 'They died.' He looked around the therapy room. 'Where are the gas and masks? Let's get this over with.'

Illraya dropped her hands from his shoulders and led the way to where a cabinet stood at the rear of the room. She thumbed the lock and the door opened as the mechanism recognized her thumb-print. Inside, cylinders of gas stood together with masks.

'The gas is similar to the type that you used on the mutineers,' she explained. 'It was that which gave me the idea. It is carried for controlled anaesthesia during long operations. The masks each have their own oxygen supply for use in cases of pulmonary complication.'

The apparatus was standard therapy room equipment on any ship making a long journey. She was talking to ease her own tension. Carmodine counted the cylinders.

'Will three be enough?'

'I don't know,' she admitted. 'It should be. The gas is highly compressed and is normally used with a high dilution of ordinary air. And, of course, we have direct-injection drugs which can be fired from the hypoguns.'

'If we get close enough,' he reminded.

Reaching out, he took the cylinders from their rack. They were of light-weight alloy.

'Bring the others,' he said. 'Stack them by the door. I'll see if the passage is clear.'

Carrying one of the cylinders, he tucked the gun he'd taken from the guard under his armpit as he silently opened the panel. Listening, he heard nothing. He took the gun from beneath his arm and, opening the door wide, stepped into the passage.

Three men stood in line across the passage. All were armed. As they saw him, they lifted their guns and began to fire.

13

Resurrection

Carmodine's reaction was instinctive. He yelled and threw the gas cylinder he was carrying directly at the men and, at the same time, dropped and opened fire. He heard the roar of guns, felt skin blister and smelled the stench of burning hair as flame lashed the air above, but the shots were not aimed directly at him.

Instinctively the men had aimed at the missile, unable to recognize it for what it was, trying only to blast a threat from the air. They fired and fired again. The cylinder, bathed in fire, began to fuse, the lightweight alloy softened by the savage heat. Inside, the compressed gas, heated, fought to escape.

Carmodine had time for only two shots before the cylinder exploded.

He felt the blast, heard the roar, the whine of metal. He rolled, holding his breath, rising to slam through the door of the therapy room, closing the panel tightly behind him.

Illraya stepped forward. 'Jules! What — '

He cut her short with a curt gesture, pointed to his clamped lips and then to the masks. He snatched one up and pulled it over his face, twisting the control and sending a blast of oxygen through the mouthpiece. Once more breathing regularly, he turned to Illraya. She was fumbling with the valve, eyes enormous behind the transparent visor. Carmodine knocked aside her hands and fed oxygen into the mask.

'Are you all right now?' The diaphragm set into the wall of his mask carried the words.

Illraya gulped air into her lungs. 'Yes,' she said, and added, 'What happened? I felt dizzy, ill.'

'They were waiting outside,' he explained. 'Three of them. They fired at me but hit the gas cylinder instead. It exploded in their faces. The corridor is now contaminated with the gas. It must be spreading all over. We've got to get to the air plant and finish the job.' He scooped up one of the cylinders. 'Can you manage the other one?'

He stepped out into the corridor as she nodded. The gun he aimed down the passage was unnecessary. It was empty of life. On the floor, where they had fallen, the bodies of the three men lay sprawled in death. Carmodine stared grimly at the three crystals brightly shining beneath the blood that marred their perfection.

Only the men had died. The parasites remained unharmed to live again.

If they were given the chance.

Stooping Carmodine picked up the three gems by the thongs that had supported them around the necks of their hosts. He swung them from the fingers of his left hand. The cylinder he carried beneath his left arm. He pointed with the gun he carried in his right hand.

'I'll lead the way. Try and keep an eye open for anything coming form the rear. If you spot danger, yell out and drop. Understand?'

She nodded, the mask making the gesture awkward.

Carmodine turned and moved at a run. The gas would have taken care of any immediate opposition but its distribution had been wasteful and they had lost the element of surprise. Unless they could get to the air plant before the opposition got itself organized the plan would be a flop. Spacesuits would provide protection against the gas and, given warning, the aliens could don the suits within minutes.

Carmodine rounded a corner and eased his finger on the trigger. The next passage was empty.

The one after held a slumped figure.

He jumped it, ran to the door of the air plant and turned to see Illraya trip and fall. As she rose to her feet a shape appeared at the end of the corridor.

'Down!' yelled Carmodine. 'Down!'

He fired as she flattened herself against the deck. Again as he leaped aside. Flame gushed down the corridor and spread as it enveloped the distant figure.

'Now!' Carmodine shouted the order. 'Illraya! Now!'

She rose and raced towards the door of the air plant, flung herself against it and passed through. He darted after her, turned and slammed the panel, locking it as heat blasted at the outer surface. He spun at the sound of something falling and saw Illraya standing over a slumped figure. She held a hypogun in her hand.

'He wasn't armed,' she explained. 'He tried to throw a wrench at you but I got to him first.'

'Not armed or masked,' said Carmodine. 'The gas couldn't have reached here or, if it has, it is too weak to do any good.' He lifted his fingers to tear off his mask, then thought better of it. 'No. Best not to take any chances. Let's get this gas into the air system.'

Something heavy smashed against the door as he ran toward the central blowers. It was repeated as if whoever was outside was using a heavy hammer or crowbar. The door was of relative weakness and it wouldn't be able to withstand such an attack for long. Carmodine grunted as he set down the cylinder of gas and leaned towards the humming machinery of the air system.

It was a basically simple arrangement.

Air was collected, blown through and over tanks of algae and mutated vegetation, washed and then blown back into circulation. Carmodine selected a spot on the main tube just past the fans. The head of an inspection plate carried a single large nut.

'The wrench,' he snapped to Illraya. 'Get it for me, please.'

She ran to where the unconscious man sprawled and returned with the tool. Her face looked strained as the attack on the door redoubled in fury.

'Hurry, Jules. If they get into space-suits . . .'

'I know,' he interrupted. 'Take the gun and stand by the door. Use it if you have to.'

Metal chimed as he adjusted the wrench over the head of the nut. A turn and it was loose. Quickly he spun it free, jerked away the plate and lifted one of the gas cylinders into place just beneath the opening. The blast of air through the pipe would provide more than enough suction to attract the gas and its own velocity would feed it into the pipe.

With the wrench, Carmodine cracked the valve, opened it wide and, jamming the cylinder into place, reached for the other.

He heard the scream of tearing metal, Illraya's warning cry and turned to see the battered door sagging from its hinges.

'Duck!' he shouted to the woman. 'Get out of the line of fire.'

His hands were busy as he spoke. The wrench the valve, a twist and gas shrieked from the cylinder. He turned it towards the door and flung it through the opening. From somewhere beyond, a gun fired. Then came the sound of falling bodies.

Then silence.

'They weren't in spacesuits,' said Illraya thankfully. 'Jules! We've done it!'

Carmodine stepped towards her, took the gun and peered around the opening in the door. The gas cylinder lay among a sprawl of unconscious figures. He tore open the panel and stepped towards them. Two were dead, killed by the blast he had heard, the gun probably triggered by the constriction of an unconscious finger. On their chests, dulled by their blood, crystals shone with lambent splendor. The others were anaesthetized and sprawled asleep.

One was Mason. Carmodine stooped and tugged at the thong around his neck. The crystal slipped from his blouse dull and lifeless. Carmodine poised it to wrench it clear and toss it to one side, then paused. Thoughtfully he looked at the crystals worn by the dead men, visible through their charred clothing, then at the one in his hand. The aliens had left the dead bodies, but not those simply unconscious. Why?

'They must know,' said Illraya when he asked the question. 'Somehow they must recognize the difference between death and unconsciousness, otherwise they would leave when the host was asleep.'

'Like a man riding a horse,' said Carmodine slowly. 'He can tell if the beast is dead or asleep. The heartbeat alone would tell him that.'

It was a crude analogy but good enough for a working hypothesis. Carmodine leaned back, squatting on his heels, thinking. If the aliens left their hosts when those hosts were dead, then they should leave them when death was simulated. If they didn't then they must know the signs of actual demise. And, if a man had to die in order to rid him of his parasite — ?

'No,' said Carmodine to Illraya as she began to collect the crystals from the unconscious men. 'Leave them. I have an idea.'

'To save the men?'

'I don't know if it will work,' he admitted. 'But it's worth trying because they have nothing to lose. Clinical death can last how long before deterioration sets in?'

'Three minutes is the workable period,' she said instantly. 'Five is maximum tolerance. After that the brain cells begin to deteriorate and can never be restored.' She looked at him and guessed his intention. 'Jules! Are you sure you know what you're doing?'

'Yes,' he said. 'I'm sure.'

Kneeling beside the unconscious Mason, he lowered his hands to the man's throat.

For a moment he hesitated. Press the carotids or the windpipe? Cut off the supply of blood to the brain or the supply of air to the lungs? The first was the most merciful but what cared an unconscious man about mercy? And it was easier to inflate a man's lungs than to start his heart.

Deliberately Carmodine began to throttle the engineer.

He didn't play at it. The man had saved his life but he was no longer a man. He was a thing, an alien parasite, a danger to the inner worlds. The knuckles shone white beneath the skin as Carmodine tightened his hands. Mason made a peculiar croaking sound and, unconscious though he was, stirred a little. Muscular reflex or the alien striving to save its host?

Carmodine kept squeezing. He had laid the crystal high on the engineer's throat where he could see the dull surface. Mason's face turned livid. His eyes opened and stared with a terrible blankness. He jerked as the alien fought to fill his lungs and then, abruptly, he collapsed.

The crystal flamed with shimmering glory.

Carmodine snatched it from Mason's throat and flung it against a bulkhead. He stooped, took a breath from his mask, removed the mask and placed his mouth over the engineer's and blew strongly into the empty lungs. He lifted his head back into the mask Illraya held for him, breathed, and felt the soft exhalation as Mason's chest expelled the air. Again Carmodine blew into the dead man's lungs, again and again.

Mason snorted and began to inhale in short, ragged gasps.

'You did it,' said Illraya, holding the mask over his face. 'Killed him and then brought him back to life.' She paused and added, 'Without his parasite.'

'They have a strong survival instinct,' said Carmodine. 'We can use it to our advantage. Stand by to give adrenaline and heart massage if necessary. We haven't got all that much time in which to work.' He moved to kneel beside another man. 'Keep the gun handy,' he said quietly. 'We don't want to be interrupted.'

Carmodine killed the man and then, when his crystal shone with eye-catching color, removed the gem and resurrected him.

Kerlen was next.

Then two crewmen.

Winguard.

Winguard's assistant.

Another crewman.

Another.

It became mechanical, an endles line of unconscious men who had to be killed so that they might live again. Against the bulkhead, the heap of crystals grew larger.

'That's the last one here,' said Illraya as Carmodine straightened and looked around. 'There's the man in the air plant.' She stooped over her patient and checked his pulse.

'You go and attend to him,' she said. 'I'll be able to manage out here.'

Carmodine flexed his hands and rose. He felt tired, waves of fatigue robbing his strength, his hands aching from effort. Inside the mask his face streamed with perspiration.

'Go on,' she urged. 'I can manage. Once you've taken care of him the worst is over.'

He shrugged, too tired to correct her, not wanting to spoil her sense of achievement. But they hadn't won. Not yet.

Not until every crystal in the ship had been destroyed or thrown outside. Until every parasitic life form had been eradicated from its host.

Brooding he entered the air plant.

And almost died from a thrusting lance of steel.

He caught the shimmer of light, the impression of movement and spun aside as a sharpened rod pierced the air where he had stood. The man he had come to kill was awake and determined to fight. If Carmodine lost he could not hope for resurrection.

He twisted again as light splintered from the tip of the rod. The man was amazingly fast. He darted in like a snake, thrust, was away before Carmodine could catch either man or weapon. If he only had a gun!

But Illraya had the weapon and she was busy outside.

Carmodine snarled within the mask.

An accident of tolerance, he supposed. That or the fact the man had been lying close to the opened pipe that could have sucked the contaminated air from the room. It didn't matter. Either Carmodine would overpower the man or he would be killed. Illraya had the gun but she wouldn't think of using it until it was too late.

All she would see would be a masked figure coming from the room. Carmodine had entered it wearing a mask. A man with a mask would emerge.

He would snatch the gun, knock her out and prime her with a crystal. Prime them all.

And, this time, there could be no second chance.

The rod thrust again, handled as if it were a foil. Carmodine avoided the lunge by luck and judgment. The luck couldn't last. Unless he acted fast he would be as good as dead.

The next thrust he parried with a wild sweep of his arm. Racing forward he knocked the lance to one side and snatched at the exhausted gas cylinder.

Dodging he felt the acid burn of steel in his side, the sudden warmth as blood gushed from the wound. Desperately he flung the cylinder. The man sprang to one side. Carmodine dropped one hand to the lance, gripped, lifted the other to pull the mask from his head. As he flung it at the man, he jerked the lance free of the man's grip, tore it from his side and, reversing it, stabbed the sharp tip directly into the man's heart.

And watched the crystal the man was wearing flame into shining brilliance.

Tiredly, Carmodine stooped to snatch it from where it rested, trying not to see the dull, accusing eyes. A little more foresight and the man would now be alive and free of the parasite that had usurped his body. But if it was too late to save him at least he could be avenged.

Savagely Carmodine smashed the heel of his boot against the crystal. It slipped, unharmed, to one side. Snatching up the wrench he hammered at the shining surface, pounding it with the full strength of his arms and shoulders! Agony flared through his temples as the thing suddenly shattered into a scatter of lifeless dust. Dropping the wrench, he clutched his head, groaning, feeling as if the naked surface of his brain had been seared with acid.

After a long while the pain died.

Shuddering, Carmodine wiped the sweat from his face and rose slowly to his feet. A defence mechanism, he guessed. The parasites were not wholly without protection. No wonder the memory of such agony, multiplied as it must have been, had been enough to create amnesia on his first voyage.

That and other things.

Carmodine sucked in a deep breath, realizing that the air was untainted by gas and, that if any others were in the ship, they would have to be found immediately. And he knew there must be at least one other.

Brensco had not been among those they had met in the corridor.

He felt a tingle of fear and turned towards the door. There was no sound from the passage yet surely Illraya must have heard the sounds of the fight?

Certainly she must have heard the noise as he hammered the crystal. Carmodine stepped quietly to the door of the air plant and looked outside.

Illraya had gone.

He stepped forward, eyes searching the passage. He could see the mask she had worn lying to one side. The dead lay where they had fallen. The crystals he had thrown aside still rested in a little heap at the foot of a bulkhead. The men he had freed from their alien parasites were still unconscious where they had been drawn into line. He jumped through the door, turning in mid-air so that he landed facing back the way he had come. The bulkhead to either side of the door was empty.

Carmodine relaxed a little. The woman had probably just left and would be back in a moment. But why hadn't she told him? Why discard her mask?

He remembered the savage agony in his temples when he had shattered the crystal. She could have looked in, seen him in pain and rushed to get something to help. The mask? The gas had dissipated or the oxygen flask had become exhausted.

Illraya would probably be back in the therapy room.

Carmodine headed towards it, striding down the passage to the junction, turning down it, hurrying so as to catch up with the woman. A door stood half-open down the corridor. He slowed as he neared it, glanced inside as he drew level and came to a sudden halt.

'Illraya!' He stepped into the room. 'Illraya!'

She didn't answer. She rested supine on the bunk, her face pale against the copper aureole of her hair, eyes closed as if asleep or unconscious. On the bare flesh of her throat, a crystal shone in flaming splendor.

Carmodine sprang forward to snatch it away.

'Do not touch it! If you do, I will kill you!'

Carmodine froze, ice water drenching his brain with the realization of his own stupidity. Slowly he turned, keeping both hands extended and in full view.

Brensco stared at him over the barrel of a gun.

14

The end of Brensco

The man looked ill. His blue eyes were red with broken capillaries and his face was haggard. He looked like a man who has worked too hard, too long — or had been driven to the point of physical exhaustion by an uncaring parasite.

'You!' Carmodine lowered his hands a little. 'You've been outside,' he said. 'That's why you didn't come running with the others.'

'Your assumption is correct,' said the Brensco-alien in a flat, emotionless voice. 'While you were busy I was outside gathering our cargo. It took longer than I had anticipated, but the fact that I was sealed from the gas you had released enabled me to remain mobile.' He gestured with the gun in his hand. 'You will move to one side. I do not wish to injure the female should I decide to use this weapon.'

'Kill me, you mean?' Carmodine stepped to one side and a shade closer to the entity in Brensco's body. 'Because I smashed one of your damned crystals to dust?'

An expression almost of anger suffused Brensco's ravaged features. 'An act for which you will pay. We are too few for such as you to be permitted to destroy any of our number. The Elder Race must not be endangered by animals. We have waited too long for suitable hosts and further risks must not be taken.' The alien poised the gun, aiming at Carmodine's stomach. 'I think it best to dispose of you now.'

'Wait!' Carmodine stepped a trifle closer. 'Wouldn't it be foolish to kill me? Are you so certain you can do without my knowledge?' He relaxed a little as the alien held its fire. 'I know how you must operate,' he said quickly. 'I know that you merge into a symbiosis with your host. No,' he corrected himself. 'Not a symbiosis because you give nothing in return for what you take. You occupy the full mind and body of a man, but do you also gain full mastery of his skill? Can you operate this vessel?'

The gun lowered a little. 'You are shrewd,' said the alien. 'You are correct in what you assume. I have access to the memories and knowledge of this man, but finer points of control as yet elude me. It is not important. There will be time to learn.'

'If you allow him to live that long,' said Carmodine harshly. 'A man needs food and water, rest and recreation, exercise and sleep if he is to remain efficient. You things never sleep. You don't know how to use the strength of the body you wear. To you it's just a machine to be used and replaced when necessary. But if you hope to land this vessel, you need more than simple muscle.'

'If necessary I can release control,' said the alien. 'Let the man resume his normal life if necessary at critical intervals. Allow him to operate the vessel when needed.'

'If he would be willing,' said Carmodine. 'How can you be certain of that?'

'There must be no doubt.' Something flared in the blank eyes. 'We have waited too long to be thwarted now.'

'And the Elder Race are few and can not breed. Is that it?'

'You know?'

'I guessed,' said Carmodine. He inched forward a little more. 'It is obvious that the crystalline shape must be artificial. What happened?'

'You are curious,' said the alien. 'It is a thing I can appreciate, for I too am a seeker of knowledge. Know this, then. Long ago, how long it is impossible to calculate now, this world was fertile and we of the Elder Race walked as men. I say walked as men, but we were not human, for we were intelligent entities that had entered upon a symbiotic relationship with a race of beasts. We provided the brain, the intelligence and the animal gave us motive power in return. More. With their aid, we could construct and manipulate various mechanisms and devices. Over the course of time, the beasts could not survive without our aid, so low had their individual awareness become.

'Time passed and something happened

to the Sun. It changed, altered, and the outer worlds grew cold. Our hosts died and we died with them. We had knowledge of science, but lacked both the skill and the means to travel to other worlds. In desperation our men of knowledge devised a plan. They manufactured new bodies for us, which could withstand the cold and other hardships. We left the dying bodies of our hosts and entered the new containers. Our hosts died, but we did not die. We rested on the frozen surface of this planet, waiting for something to reverse what had happened to the Sun, for new forms of life to emerge so that we could take over their bodies as we had of old.'

Waiting, thought Carmodine bleakly. Trapped in the crystals, impervious to the passage of time. Waiting for how long? Eons, at least. Climatic cycles. An incredible length of time when measured against the life-expectancy of men. A flicker of duration when measured against the eternal universe.

'We came,' he said quietly. 'The men of the first expedition.'

'Our first contact,' said the alien. 'And now you have arrived again.' Triumph flared in the bloodshot eyes. 'From the memories of this host I have learned that the inner planets are filled with more like yourselves. Uncountable numbers of adaptable hosts. With their aid, the Elder Race shall live again. We will return with you and, later, other ships will land on this planet. They will take back more of us. And more. Until there are none left here and the caverns are empty. And then we shall rule until the end of time.'

Carmodine shook his head. 'No,' he said. 'You can stop dreaming. That simply isn't going to happen.'

'I say it will and there is nothing you can do to prevent it, nothing you can say or do which will turn me from the path that must be followed.'

'You are inconsistent,' said Carmodine. 'The body you are wearing is poisoned with fatigue. Your intelligence has become contaminated with toxic matter.'

The Brensco-alien lifted the gun and aimed it at Carmodine's chest. 'I know what you are relying on,' it said flatly, 'but you are not thinking with precision. The hosts you have freed of the dominance of the Elder Race can be redominated. They will help operate this vessel. So will the host I inhabit. I have refrained from destroying you for the sake of your body that would serve as a host also, and for the sake of your skills. These things have lost their relative importance. Your elimination is preferable to the risk attendant on leaving you alive.'

The muzzle of the gun lifted a little. 'So I am going to kill you now.'

Carmodine tensed, crouching a little as he flexed the muscles of his calves and thighs. His only hope rested in the fact that Brensco was unaccustomed to firearms. The thing that had taken over the blond man's body, that is. It would be a little unsure as to how hard to press the trigger, a little doubtful as to the effect of the shot. It would linger, searching borrowed memories, able to afford the luxury of taking its time.

Paul, he remembered, had always betrayed a sadistic streak.

'You are thinking that you will be able

to avoid the shot,' said the alien. 'You are thinking that you may be able to avoid injury and hurt this host in turn. As there is a remote possibility that such a thing could happen, you will walk ahead of me into the corridor.'

Carmodine bared his teeth. 'Go to Hell.'

'I warn you that I shall not hesitate to fire if you do not immediately obey. My only object is to save the possibility of injury to the female.'

'You don't want to hurt a precious host, is that it?'

Carmodine sneered. 'To Hell with what you want! If you're going to kill me then go right ahead. Why should I do anything you want me to do? You aliens must be crazy!'

During the shouting he had shifted his weight a little. He would have to wait until the very last moment and then he would duck and throw his body forward against Brensco's legs. With any sort of luck at all the first shot would miss incapacitating him. The second . . . ?

He didn't think of that. A man could

only ask for just so much luck at a time. If he could manage to dodge the first shot, the rest would be strictly up to himself alone. If he didn't, then nothing else would ever matter again.

But he had to time his move exactly right.

He watched the hand gripping the butt of the heavy weapon, the fingers, the knuckles, the fingernails. With a man he would have watched the eyes, but Brensco was no longer a man and so he watched the one thing he could trust. The slowly whitening knuckle of the trigger finger.

'Captain!' The voice came from the corridor, grew louder as footsteps approached. Mason drew level with the open door of the cabin and looked inside. 'Captain! What — '

The alien turned and fired all in one quick motion. The engineer shrieked, clawing at his smoking side, spinning as he tried to avoid the blast. He slammed into the corridor wall, blood staining his hands as he tried to staunch the wound.

Carmodine lunged forward, his left

hand gripping Brensco's wrist, his right snatching at the barrel of the gun. He twisted the weapon against Brensco's hand, trapping the trigger finger, tearing the gun free as he snapped the bone.

The alien turned before Carmodine could use the gun, its left hand slashing at Carmodine's eyes as, with the right, it snatched at the gun. The gun fell to the deck as Carmodine tossed it clear and then, suddenly, he was fighting a panther and weapons were forgotten in the savage heat of primitive combat.

Both men were skilled in the art of combat. Both men had muscles tempered by years of active use and both men fought for something greater than their own lives. But where Carmodine was a man, with a man's feeling for pain and injury, Brensco's body was possessed by an alien who could feel no hurt.

Brensco's face remained cold, expressionless as the alien chopped the edge of a stiffened hand across the bridge of Carmodine's nose. The broken finger didn't seem to bother it. It hit with the left hand, a cruel blow to the pit of

Carmodine's stomach, and then raked at his eyes with the hooked fingers of the right hand.

Carmodine grunted as he felt the cartilage yield and tasted blood from his broken nose. He doubled over as pain lanced from his stomach, then desperately threw back his head to save his eyes. The clawing fingers ripped skin from his cheek, the little finger slipping into his open mouth. Carmodine bit down, felt something crunch and spat out a mouthful of blood.

Grimly he pounded Brensco's body with his big fists, using the entire strength of his arms, back and shoulders. The alien made little attempt to defend itself, seeming content to take punishment as long as it could give it. It was an unfair exchange. The alien could feel nothing, it was only its envelope that was being hurt, and, on top of that, its strength was frightening.

Carmodine cried out as a fist smashed against his ribs and he felt the stabbing agony of broken bone. Jagged ends tore at delicate tissue, filling his chest with liquid fire, his throat with the saltiness of blood. A thumb gouged at his eyes as a stamping foot rasped down his shin and hammered on his instep. Fire exploded from his groin and he doubled over, retching, as a hand chopped at the side of his throat.

The alien loomed above him, blue eyes staring from the pulped ruin of Brensco's face. It drew back a foot and kicked with cold deliberation. Carmodine groaned as agony washed from his injured side. He rolled to protect himself, looking at Brensco's body through a fog of pain, arms and legs twitching as he fought to control his injured tissues.

The alien lifted a foot for the finishing blow.

Carmodine watched as it came. He saw the boot swing back and then dart forward directly to a point between his eyes. It would smash his skull, drive the splintered fragments back into the brain, spilling his life in a mess of red and grey.

Somewhere inside of his body the primitive urge to survive overrode physical agony. All his strength and desperation went into one final effort.

He caught the boot with hands slippery with blood. He caught it — and twisted.

Brensco toppled, hopelessly off-balance, trying to spin his body in an effort to release the trapped limb. Carmodine staggered to his feet, the boot still within his hands and with a final effort, wrenched the foot in a circle about the axis of the ankle.

The sound of the hip joint breaking was like the snap of muffled wood.

Brensco dropped, hands clawing at the deck, his face expressionless beneath the mask of blood. Watching him Carmodine felt physically ill. No normal man could have fought on with such injuries. But Brensco wasn't human. He writhed like a crippled spider as he hunched along the plates as if trying to regain his feet.

Mason recognized the danger.

The engineer had been lying huddled against the wall of the corridor, fighting the pain of his wound, the gush of blood from the seared flesh. Now he lifted himself on one elbow and yelled at Carmodine. 'The gun! He's after the gun!'

The weapon Carmodine had torn free

from Brensco's broken hand and thrown aside. He looked for it and saw the heavy thing lying at the foot of the bunk. He threw himself at it just as the alien reached the weapon, the impetus of his body flattening the pistol between them.

Fire blasted from the gun as Brensco's finger closed on the trigger.

Carmodine felt the blast sear his chest, smoking as it lashed past his face, filling his nostrils with the odor of charred flesh and burned hair. He coughed, and, in a sudden panic wiped his eyes. Retinal images danced in flaring reds and yellows, giant sunflowers wheeling against an infinity of dark.

But he wasn't blind. In a short while he could see.

Brensco was dead. The blast had been directed inward by the impact of Carmodine's body. The shaft of energy had seared through the chest, smashed the crystal to ruin, passed along the base of the throat and up and outwards through the top of Brensco's skull.

Brensco was dead, but no one could ever have recognized him as the tall, blond, impeccably dressed commander of the Second Pluto Expedition.

Slowly Carmodine rose, reached out and took the crystal from Illraya's throat. It was still beautiful with shimmering radiance. The fight had taken less time than he had guessed.

'She'll be all right, Captain,' said Mason. The engineer had managed to climb to his feet and stood in the doorway. Painfully he moved to stand at the side of the bunk. 'I've seen a few fights in my time,' he mused, 'but never anything like that. For a while there, I thought it was all up for us. I couldn't do a thing to help. Then you managed to grab his foot.' He sucked in his breath. 'What's been happening, Captain?'

Carmodine looked down at the woman. She was breathing lightly, easily. Gassed, he suspected. Perhaps she had taken off the mask a little too soon or perhaps the alien had taken it off for her. Maybe she had walked into the cabin or perhaps it had carried her. It made no difference now. Soon she would wake and be able to give them all whatever treatment they needed.

Drugs to rob them of pain and things to aid healing.

He stiffened as he remembered something.

'Mason, when you woke up back there, were any of the others conscious?'

'Not that I noticed.' The engineer cocked his head, listening. 'Seems as if they must be out of it by now, though, whatever it was.' There was an odd note to his voice. 'Why, Captain? Something worrying you?'

'There are some crystals back there. I don't want anyone to touch them. If anyone disobeys my order this time, I will personally shoot him to death.'

Mason looked thoughtful. 'I saw them,' he admitted. 'Pretty things, but I wouldn't touch one with a ten-foot pole. Don't ask me why, but to me they look like snakes, poisonous ones. I guess the others will feel the same.' He noticed Carmodine's expression. 'There's something wrong, isn't there?'

Carmodine looked at the engineer. 'Don't you know?' he asked. 'Don't you remember?'

'I had a dream,' said Mason slowly. 'A

nightmare. I don't want to think about it. But it ended with you killing me, choking me to death.' He turned as footsteps echoed down the corridor. 'Here come the others. Your orders, Captain?'

'Call the men. Have them take us and Illraya to the therapy room. Have them collect any crystals they might find and stack them by the airlock. Same with the bodies of the dead.'

'I understand, sir.'

He probably did, at that, thought Carmodine. Sometimes it was best not to remember too much. Not when it touched on matters of discipline or threw doubts on loyalty. But the past could be forgotten. The evidence available would serve to reinstate him with both the Federation and the Homogenetic League. He and Illraya would have each other. The men would retain their freedom.

But before they left Pluto, he would make a personal search of every nook and cranny in the entire vessel to make sure no crystals would be riding to the inner worlds. No alien life.

He would have a clean ship.

We do hope that you have enjoyed reading this large print book.

Did you know that all of our titles are available for purchase?

We publish a wide range of high quality large print books including:
Romances, Mysteries, Classics
General Fiction
Non Fiction and Westerns

Special interest titles available in large print are:
The Little Oxford Dictionary
Music Book, Song Book
Hymn Book, Service Book

Also available from us courtesy of Oxford University Press:
Young Readers' Dictionary
(large print edition)
Young Readers' Thesaurus
(large print edition)

For further information or a free brochure, please contact us at:
Ulverscroft Large Print Books Ltd.,
The Green, Bradgate Road, Anstey,
Leicester, LE7 7FU, England.
Tel: (00 44) **0116 236 4325**
Fax: (00 44) **0116 234 0205**

Other titles in the
Linford Mystery Library:

RICOCHET

J. F. Straker

John Everard is a cold, ruthless businessman. When he returns home from a business trip he discovers that his Spanish wife Juanita and baby son Tommy have disappeared, his house has been burgled, and his firm's payroll stolen. Moreover, it was his wife who was seen driving the thieves away in Everard's own Jaguar. Has Juanita been kidnapped — or is she implicated in the robbery? And where is Tommy? Now, with little police co-operation, Everard begins his own investigation . . .

FOOL'S PARADISE

John Russell Fearn

In a fit of pique, Milly Morton — confidential 'secretary' to industrialist Mortimer Bland — deliberately smashed the astronomical plates of Bland's Chief Scientist, Anton Drew. Furthermore, she'd destroyed data which would warn the world of a forthcoming cosmic disaster. The unprecedented violent storms, signs of approaching doom, went unrecognized. Eventually Drew, aided by his friends Ken and Thayleen West, convinced the Prime Minister of the danger — but would it be too late to save the world?

DEATH COMES CALLING

John Glasby

In Los Angeles, the wealthy Marcia Edwards asks investigator Johnny Merak to find her missing grandson. Merak suspects it's a mob kidnapping. There's someone else who wants to hire him: the model Angela Cliveden, who has been receiving life-threatening phone calls. Merak discovers that she is the girlfriend of Tony Minello of the local Mafia. But when she is found murdered in her apartment, Merak is trapped in a potential Mob War and matching his wits with a cunning serial killer.